C F
HART-AL Anna's
Hart Alison.
Anna's blizzard /
1068885654
WORN, SOILED, OBSOLETE
WOODWARD, OBSOLETE

WITHDRAWN

D0252762

Anna's
Blizzard

CP
JR
A Peachtree Junior Publication

Published by
PEACHTREE PUBLISHERS
1700 Chattahoochee Avenue
Atlanta, Georgia 30318-2112

www.peachtree-online.com

Text © 2005 by Alison Hart
Illustrations © 2005 by Paul Bachem

All rights reserved. No part of this publication may be reproduced, stored in a retrieval system, or transmitted in any form or by any means—electronic, mechanical, photocopy, recording, or any other—except for brief quotations in printed reviews, without the prior permission of the publisher.

Cover design by Loraine Joyner
Book design by Melanie McMahon Ives

Manufactured in China
10 9 8 7 6 5 4 3 2 1
First Edition

Library of Congress Cataloging-in-Publication Data

Hart, Alison.
  Anna's blizzard / by Alison Hart.-- 1st ed.
    p. cm.
  Summary: Having never excelled at schoolwork, twelve-year-old Anna discovers that she may know a few things about survival when the 1888 Children's Blizzard traps her and her classmates in their Nebraska schoolhouse.
  Includes bibilographical references
  ISBN 1-56145-349-8
  [1. Survival--Fiction. 2. Blizzards--Fiction. 3. Schools--Fiction. 4. Nebraska--History--19th century--Fiction.] I. Title.
  PZ7.H256272Ar 2005
  [Fic]--dc22
                                        2005010825

Anna's Blizzard

written by *Alison Hart*

PEACHTREE
ATLANTA

To

brave

girls

everywhere

—A. H.

TABLE OF CONTENTS

CHAPTER ONE

Nebraska—January 12, 1888

Get along now, sheep." Leaning down from her pony Top Hat, Anna Vail swatted a woolly back with a coil of rope. The sheep trotted on spindly legs toward the gate leading into the pasture. Their small hooves tapped the frozen sod. Their bleats filled the crisp air.

Suddenly, a shadow swooped across a white patch of snow.

Anna glanced up. *Hawk!* Her gloved fingers tensed on the reins as the startled flock surged away from the gate. Top Hat darted after them, throwing Anna onto his rump. She grabbed a hunk of mane as he swung right, circling the small herd. The sheep flowed left like a puddle of spilled milk. When they threatened to miss the gate opening, Top pinned his ears and nipped them through.

Anna pushed the gate closed behind the retreating sheep. As she secured it with the coil of rope, she blew a frosty breath.

"You almost unseated me chasing those silly critters, Top." She patted the pony's neck. "Now we best hurry home or Mama will have a fit."

Top broke into a jog, jostling Anna on his bare back. She tightened her legs against the pony's sides, fuzzy with winter hair. Her calf-length skirt hiked up around her knees. She wore a jacket and the wool stockings, cap, scarf, and wristlets that Mama had knitted. All were itchy. All smelled like sheep, but they kept her warm.

Top trotted quickly through a snowdrift left over from the last storm. For the past two days it had been unusually warm, and prairie grass poked through the melting snow.

It's almost like spring's arrived, Anna thought. But she knew better. Nebraska winters often lingered through April. She'd even heard tales of frost in July.

Top's gait quickened when he spotted the windmill

and the barn that meant home. Minutes later, Anna spied Mama, a speck in the front of the sod house. She was waving in Anna's direction.

"Uh oh. Mama's on the lookout. She'll blister my backside if I'm late again for school," Anna told Top. Slackening the rein, she urged the pony into a canter.

Every morning after a breakfast of cornmeal mush, Anna and Top cared for the sheep. In spring, summer, and fall, they followed the herd as the sheep grazed on the unfenced land. But in winter they had to go to school.

"I'd rather be herding sheep, Papa," Anna had protested.

But Mama had insisted. "Anna's eleven years old now," she'd told Papa. "This winter she needs to spend more time with scholars and less time with critters."

Mama just didn't understand. Sheep didn't giggle when Anna misspelled "state" or stumbled over addition facts.

Flicking his ears, Top cantered past the sheep shed and pen. Anna reined him around a patch of prairie dog holes. Then she aimed the pony toward the fire ditch that circled the house and barn.

She whooped as Top leaped the ditch and careened into the yard of the sod house. Mama was backing out the front door, tugging a ticking-striped mattress. Anna's four-year-old brother, Little Seth, was in the doorway pushing at the other end.

Top threw up his head at the sight and skidded to a halt. Anna shot over his neck, landing heels over head in the flock of chickens, which squawked and flapped in all directions.

Jumping to her feet, she hooted, "Hoowee. That was some dismount!"

"Anna Vail, that is no way for a lady to conduct herself," Mama scolded as she and Seth leaned the mattress against the outside wall of the soddy.

Turning, Mama propped her fists on her hips. The frayed hem of her long skirt swept the ground. A woolen shawl hung from her shoulders and a scarf peeked from under her bonnet.

"Oh, don't worry, Mama," Anna said. "That little tumble didn't hurt a bit."

"I'm speaking of your school dress and jacket. Covered with prairie dirt. Just like everything else in this godforsaken land." Mama, born and bred in Virginia, pined for green grass, tall oaks, and rolling mountains.

Anna hurriedly brushed off her skirt.

"Now get a move on, young lady," Mama continued

to scold. "I'll not have Miss Simmons calling on me again to complain of your tardiness."

"Yes ma'am." As Anna hurried into the house, she flung her long braid over one shoulder and righted her knit cap.

The Vails' soddy consisted of two rooms. A small family bedroom took up the back of the house. In the front room, where they spent most of their time, there was a glass-pane window, a luxury on the prairie. Framed pictures and an oval mirror hung on the white-washed walls. A stove stood in the middle. Beside it was a basket of wood and two rocking chairs.

To the right of the stove were a kitchen table, cupboard, sink, and counter. Sacks of fried corn, dried beans, and onions hung in one corner. Shelves filled with canning jars and crocks lined the walls.

Anna grabbed her lunch pail, tablet, and slate off the kitchen table, then hurried back outside. Top stood stiff-legged, eyeing Little Seth, who was dragging a quilt across the yard. Little Seth was too young for school, so he stayed home to help with chores.

Anna wished mightily that *she* could stay home.

"Today would surely be a good day for cleaning the sheep shed," she said to Mama as she slid the slate and tablet under her jacket.

"Might be, but you're going to school." Hands still on her hips, Mama closed her eyes and tilted her chin toward the morning sun. "Almost like spring's in the air," she murmured, the golden light softening the lines in her face. "It's a shame it'll never last." She opened her eyes. "At least we have a good day to air the mattresses and pick lice."

Anna perked up. Picking lice was a heap better than doing sums. "I can help!"

"No, missy, you will not. Little Seth and I will wrestle the vermin. You will triumph over grammar rules."

Anna's shoulders slumped. Mama was not giving way. And she couldn't look to Papa for sympathy either. He had left early that morning, heading into town during this break in the cold weather for much-needed supplies. Anna wished she'd hidden in the wagon bed and gone with him.

With a sigh, Anna looped the lunch pail handle over her arm. Grabbing Top's mane, she vaulted onto the pony's back.

"Goodbye, Little Seth," she called.

"Bye, Anna Bandanna!" Twirling a rope over his head, her little brother took off after the chickens, as if trying to round them up.

Mama fixed a stern gaze on Anna. "No dallying this

morning, and keep your cap snug over your ears. This weather is as deceiving as your father when he convinced me to move out West."

"Yes ma'am," Anna replied politely. But as soon as she trotted from Mama's sight, she tore off her cap, shook out her long braid, and kicked Top into a canter. Mama might long for life far from the Nebraska plains, but not Anna. Like Papa, she loved the prairie whether it was bristling with summer heat or buried under winter snow.

In no time, Anna reached the Friesens' house. The Friesens were their closest neighbors. Her friend John Jacob and his older sister Ida had already left for school. Mr. and Mrs. Friesen were in the front yard of their soddy, surrounded by their milk cow, a turkey, and a passel of little Friesens. They stood still, as if they were posing for the traveling photographer.

"Fine day!" Mr. Friesen called.

Anna waved as Top trotted past. *Seems everyone is enjoying the day,* she told herself. *Why do I have to go to school?*

She guided Top past the Friesens' shed and down the dirt lane. It followed alongside the new barbed wire fence that enclosed the Baxters' pastures. The schoolhouse was a mile in the distance.

Ding, ding, ding. The morning bell rang across the prairie.

Anna nudged Top into a gallop. During the last snow, Papa had read aloud from *Wild Bill's Last Trail.* Mama had clucked her disapproval at the dime novel. But Anna and Little Seth, sprawled on the rag rug at Papa's feet, had listened wide-eyed. Now Anna pictured herself chasing after outlaws, just like Buffalo Bill.

The sun was a yellow polka dot when Top Hat cantered into the schoolyard. Several girls jumped rope. A circle of children was playing Poison Snake. John Jacob was tugging Eloise Baxter's hand, trying to pull her into the circle. If Eloise stepped on the "snake," a rag in the middle, she'd "die" of poison.

Anna halted Top in front of the school. She could tell from John Jacob's soot-covered face that he'd arrived early to fire up the stove. Now he was laughing and his cheeks were red beneath the black smudges. Anna waved but John Jacob was too busy pulling on Eloise, who was squealing like a caught pig.

Eloise was Anna's age, and too stuck-up to wave. She was dressed in a green velvet cloak and matching hat. Since the Baxters had a maid, Eloise had no chores, and she was always at school early enough to play.

"Mornin'," Anna called as she steered Top around the circle. No one paid her any mind. She blew out a frosty breath, telling herself she didn't care.

The second bell rang. Anna trotted Top behind the school and past the lean-to used for storing wood and cow chips. "Whoa now, pony." Sliding off his back, she tugged the headstall over his ears. The bit fell from his mouth. She looped a soft rope around his neck and tethered him to a stake near Champ, Eloise Baxter's fancy saddle horse.

Champ nickered, glad for company. In reply, Top pinned his ears, swung his hind end around, and switched his tail menacingly.

Anna snorted. "Would you quit trying to show Champ who's boss?" she scolded, sounding like Mama. She went over and patted Champ's silky neck. Eloise had left her beautiful horse bridled and saddled, his reins tied to a lone cottonwood tree.

Anna frowned at the other girl's thoughtlessness. "Least I can do is loosen your girth," she told Champ as she let it down two notches.

Then she gave Top's muzzle a quick kiss goodbye. "See you at recess."

With bridle and lunch pail in hand, Anna ran around the side of the sod building. The schoolyard was empty.

She halted on the stoop in front of the closed wooden door. *Late again.* Miss Simmons would surely be angry.

A chill wind ruffled the hairs poking from Anna's braid. Looking north, she noticed dark clouds gathering on the horizon. The weather was already changing.

Anna shivered. She hoped for snow, but only after Papa got home from his journey into town, Mama and Little Seth had finished their chores, and the sheep were safe in their pen.

With one last, longing glance across the prairie, Anna opened the schoolhouse door and stepped inside.

Chapter Two

"You're late again, Anna," Ida Friesen whispered. The older girl stood by the door, an open book in her hands. Ida was fourteen, and already looked a woman. The hem of her woolen dress brushed the dirt floor. Her brown hair was pulled into a bun.

"One day soon you will be a lady," Mama often warned Anna. If being a lady meant cumbersome skirts and prickly hairpins, Anna wanted no part of it.

Ida shut the door behind Anna. Without looking up from her book she added, "Miss Simmons won't be pleased."

Anna ducked her head. Hurrying to a dark corner, she hung the bridle on a peg and set her lunch pail underneath. Then she pulled off her gloves and wristlets and tucked them in her pockets. When she unbuttoned her jacket, her tablet and slate clattered to the wood floor.

Anna stiffened. She peeked over her shoulder. Two rows of wooden benches stretched on either side of a cast-iron stove. Boys sat on the left side, girls on the right. The school's one window and a kerosene lamp cast the only light. Still, Anna could see that all heads were turned. All eyes were on her.

Beyond the turned heads Anna could see the new blackboard, purchased with funds raised by the towns-folk. And in front of the blackboard stood Miss Simmons.

"Thank you for gracing us with your presence, Miss Vail," Miss Simmons said with tart politeness. Several of the girls tittered. A few boys guffawed.

Anna didn't bother making up a yarn. She'd already tried tales of thrown horseshoes and busted reins. Miss Simmons was from back East and had never ridden a horse, but she always managed to see through Anna's fibs.

Anna picked up her tablet and slate and hung her jacket alongside the others. Chin tucked, she scurried to the right front bench. Miss Simmons had placed Anna between Carolina and Sally Lil. Both were eight years old. Both could read, write, and cipher better than Anna.

"Scholars, please stand for the opening song," Miss Simmons said. "We will now sing 'The Star-Spangled Banner'."

The students rose. Anna slid her slate and tablet beneath the bench and stood up. Hands clasped in front of her, she sang out, "O say, can you see, by the dawn's early light, *when so loudly it hail'd* at the twilight's last glea-ming?"

Carolina nudged her hard in the ribs. "Those aren't the words," she hissed.

"Who says?" Anna hissed back. "Didn't it hail just three days ago?"

When the song was finished, Anna held on extra long to the last note. Miss Simmons gave her an impatient look before addressing the class. "Thank you, scholars. Miss Friesen will read from the Scriptures."

Ida Friesen and Eloise Baxter sat on the bench behind Anna. Eloise's father, Mr. Archibald Baxter, was the school director for the district. Miss Simmons boarded at the Baxters' house, which was two stories and built from wood. And if that wasn't enough to make her too big for her britches, Eloise always wore stylish dresses made by her mother's seamstress, who lived in the big town of Omaha.

Ida made her way up the aisle and stood beside the

teacher. In a clear voice, she read, "Job 28:12. And where is the place of understanding? Man knoweth not…"

Ida's as tall as Miss Simmons, Anna thought. Last October, she'd overheard Papa and Mama talking about "the new school ma'am from the East." Mama said she was just a child. Papa said she wouldn't last a Nebraska winter. So far the teacher had made it through three months and two snows. But this morning she looked a bit peaked.

Could be her corset, Anna decided, noting Miss Simmons's tiny waist and billowy skirts. Even Mama had discarded her petticoats and corset stays.

"Thank you, Miss Friesen. That was beautiful reading." Miss Simmons smiled as Ida walked back to the bench.

Anna cast a look at John Jacob, who sat on the boys' side in the back row. Yesterday at recess John Jacob and Karl had talked at length about Miss Simmons's pert figure and rosebud mouth. Now her best friend was staring dreamily at the teacher.

Anna rolled her eyes.

"Miss Vail?"

She swung around.

"Would you please come up to the front and lead the calisthenics?"

Anna flushed. Standing in front of the class was worse than having bedbugs in her underdrawers.

"Oh, ma'am, Top throwed me hard this morning so I doubt I can touch a toe."

Miss Simmons arched one delicate brow. "Top *threw* you this morning."

"That's right." Anna was amazed. "How'd you know?"

Giggles broke out behind her. Whirling back, Anna glared first at Eloise, then at Hattie and Ruth, sisters who also sat on the second bench and copied Eloise's every gesture.

Across the room, John Jacob raised his hand. He stood with the older boys, Karl on one side, Eugene on the other. Eugene was sixteen and had whiskers. His pa made him work sunup to sundown, so he seldom came to school.

"I'll lead the calisthenics, Miss Simmons," John Jacob offered.

"Thank you, John Jacob."

When John Jacob came up the aisle, Anna tried to catch his eye. Hadn't they spent last Saturday together hunting prairie chickens? But he kept his gaze on the teacher. *He's smitten for sure,* Anna thought crossly.

"Ready, set, and let's begin. One…two…" John Jacob recited as he bent low. On the count of three and four he stretched high.

"One, two, lamb, ewe," Anna murmured as she followed him. "Three, four, saddle sore." When she raised her arms toward the ceiling, a movement by the stovepipe caught her eye.

The schoolhouse roof was made of sod layered on top of cottonwood poles. On warm days, the melting snow dripped through the cracks between the sod slabs. Gunnysacks hung beneath the ceiling to catch any mud raining from above, but there were no sacks near the stovepipe. Dirt sprinkled down on the kettle that steamed on top of the stove.

Anna lowered her arms again and touched the tops of her laced boots. When she rose up, she spotted a furry nose poking from a hole where the stovepipe went through the roof. Before she could get a good look, the nose popped out of sight.

A mouse trying to keep warm, Anna thought. As she bent over again, she glanced past Sally Lil. The light coming through the window was as thick and gray as dirty sheep wool.

The clouds from the north must have arrived, covering the sun. Mama called them "uninvited guests." Papa called them cuss words. Anna hoped Top Hat was finding some dry grass to nibble. He'd need fodder to keep warm if the wind and the clouds brought snow.

"Thank you, John Jacob," Miss Simmons said.

John Jacob made his way back to his seat. Karl was crouched in front of the stove, stoking the fire. Each week a different family provided fuel. Anna could tell by the sound of crackling corn stalks and the smell of burning cow chips that this was the Friesens' week. With eight mouths to feed, the Friesens had no wood to spare.

"We will begin lessons now." Miss Simmons tapped on the blackboard with her pointer. "Scholars working in McGuffey's Sixth, please correct these ten sentences."

Anna straightened her spine as the other children her age pulled their tablets from under the benches. "I can read as well as they can," she muttered. She glanced at the side wall. It was covered with old sheets of the *Nebraska Farmer* newspaper to help keep out the damp.

Squinting, she read the bold letters at the top of one sheet: "Judge J. R. Giles Running for Mayor." She frowned, wondering how far the man had to run to reach Mayor, a town she'd surely never heard of.

"William and George," said Miss Simmons, directing her attention to the two smallest boys. "Miss Friesen will set your copy."

Ida often helped the teacher with the youngest boys.

She'd write several letters on their slates, and the boys would use corn kernels to outline them. "Such easy work," Anna had scoffed to Little Seth when he'd tried the same task at the kitchen table at home. "Why, I mastered my letters last school year!"

"Third Readers please join me at the recitation table," said the teacher.

Sally Lil and Carolina bounced from the bench. Skipping to the table, they sat on the two stools closest to the teacher. Anna dragged her feet and slid slowly onto the stool nearest the wall.

Miss Simmons held out a book with a fancy cover. Books were scarce on the prairie, and this gold-bound one looked especially precious.

"This is *Poetry for Children,*" Miss Simmons told them. "You will each choose a poem to memorize. Tomorrow you will recite your piece for the class."

Sallie Lil clapped her hands. Carolina beamed.

Anna wrinkled her forehead. "Ma'am. May I recite a piece from *Wild Bill's Last Trail* instead?"

"Dime novels are *not* literature, Miss Vail." The teacher set the book on the table. "Now, gently turn the pages and graciously share the poems while I look over the others' grammar lessons."

As soon as Miss Simmons walked away, Carolina snatched up the book. "Oh, these are such wondrous poems!" she exclaimed as she flipped through.

"Let me see." Sallie Lil crowded closer. The little girl's hair had been hacked off and it stuck up in tufts. That meant only one thing: lice.

Anna scooted her stool a little farther away.

"Listen, Anna, here's a poem just for you." Clearing her throat, Carolina read aloud: "Little Anna, of all my friends I like her best, not because she is pretty or handsomely dressed; Nor is she as smart as the others I know—"

"Stop your meanness!" Anna grabbed the book.

Carolina held tightly. "I'm not through." They tugged, ripping a page.

Sallie Lil gasped. Carolina dropped the book on the table. Her mouth formed a perfect O. *An O for ornery,* Anna thought, knowing that *she,* not Carolina, would get in trouble.

"Miss Simmons!" Carolina whined. "Anna tore a page in your new book!"

The teacher hurried over. "Oh, Anna!" she exclaimed when she saw the ragged piece sticking from the closed cover.

Anna jumped off the stool. Miss Simmons had *tears* in her eyes. Because of a book!

"I'm s-s-sorry," Anna stammered. "I didn't rip it on purpose."

"I would *hope* not." Miss Simmons picked it up and stroked the cover. "The book was a present."

"From a *gentleman?*" Sallie Lil asked wistfully.

"No, Sallie Lil. It was a going-away present. From one of my teachers in Boston. She gave it to me when she heard I was hired to teach…" There was a catch in her voice, and her face grew sorrowful. "…when I was hired to teach *here.*"

Anna thought of Mama. Did Miss Simmons pine for Boston like Mama pined for Virginia?

Just then a gust of wind rattled the windowpanes. The sheets of newspaper rippled. The flame in the kerosene lamp flickered.

Miss Simmons paled.

Anna hurried over to the window. The glass was slick with ice. She rubbed a hole in the frost and peered outside. In the sky, dark clouds churned like waves on a stormy river. On the plain, the bristly grass bowed like churchgoers on Sunday.

Miss Simmons came up beside her. "My, how the wind is blowing," she whispered.

"It's blowing something fierce," Anna replied. Then she lowered her voice, too, so the little girls wouldn't hear. "Miss Simmons, I don't want to worry you none, but I believe we're in for a snowstorm!"

CHAPTER THREE

Miss Simmons nodded. One hand went to her high-necked collar. The other clutched the book to her blouse buttons. Finally she said, "I've survived two Nebraska snows, Anna. And we do have plenty of snow in Boston. So I guess one more storm won't ruin me."

"Yes ma'am." Anna craned her neck, trying to see Top. But he was tethered out of sight behind the school.

"Now it's time to get back to learning," Miss Simmons reminded her. "I expect you to choose a suitable poem, Anna. Perhaps one about snow. And no more ripped pages, please."

"Oh, no ma'am. Never again."

"Scholars!" Miss Simmons turned, her skirts rustling like sheep in the straw. "Keep working on your language lessons. It will soon be time for penmanship."

Ugh, Anna thought. *I'd rather clean out a hog shed than work on penmanship.* Anna sat back on the stool. Patiently, she waited for Sally Lil and Carolina to quit arguing over poems. The air in the small room was heavy with the smell of wet wool, musty earth, dirty necks, and smoldering cow chips.

Anna yawned. She'd been up since five o'clock. She'd had to feed the chickens and collect eggs before driving the sheep to the pasture. She rested her head on her hand. Her eyes drifted shut.

In an instant she and Top Hat were racing across the prairie. Beside her Eloise and Champ tried to keep up. Long-legged Champ was no match for the plucky Top. And when Champ tripped over a grassy hummock and Eloise tumbled off, why Anna just had to…

"Anna?" Someone tapped her shoulder, and she snapped upright. Was it time to feed the chickens already?

"I believe I found you the perfect poem," Miss Simmons said, handing Anna a sheet of paper.

Blinking sleepily, Anna stared at it.

"It's by Ralph Waldo Emerson. There are some difficult words, but give it a try."

"Why, thank you, Miss Simm-m-mp—" Anna clapped her hand to her mouth, stifling another yawn.

She wanted to appear pleased, not weary. She looked down at the poem, written in the teacher's trim script.

Lips moving, Anna began to read, stumbling over the hard words as the wind shook the panes behind her:

Announced by all the trumpets of the sky
Arrives the snow, and, driving o'er the fields,
Seems nowhere to alight: the whited air
Hides hills and woods, the river and the heaven,
And veils the farm-house at the garden's end.

The poem seemed to go on forever. Finally, Anna pronounced the last painful word. Her head ached from all the reading. Her eyes blurred. She rubbed her throbbing temples. She wished she were home, so Mama would prescribe a spoonful of Dr. Benjamin's: a tonic for all ailments.

Miss Simmons came over to the table. Carolina and Sally Lil were still paging through the book of poems.

"What do you think?" the teacher asked Anna. "It's titled 'The Snow Storm'."

"It's a fine poem, ma'am, but I doubt I pronounced all the words correctly," Anna said politely. "It's a mite longwinded, too." She glanced up at her teacher. "And I don't believe Mister Waldo Emerson was writing about a Nebraska snowstorm. There ain't any cuss words."

"There *aren't* any cuss words," Miss Simmons corrected. But then she smiled at Anna, and for a moment, poor grammar and big words seemed less threatening. "Just memorize the first verse for tomorrow. You can work on the rest of it next week."

Anna repeated the first two lines of the poem to herself over and over. She just about had them by heart when Miss Simmons announced that it was time for penmanship. Anna clutched her stomach, wishing again for a large dose of Dr. Benjamin's.

Miss Simmons passed out the pens and ink. Anna retrieved her tablet from under the bench. Ida, Eloise, Hattie, and Ruth flounced up to the recitation table. "We can sit here because *we* are almost ladies," Eloise explained to everyone.

Almost *being a lady is a far cry from* being *one,* Anna thought sourly.

John Jacob and Karl stretched out on the plank floor. Eugene stayed on the bench and balanced his tablet on his knees. Anna and the others sat Indian style on the floor and used the benches as desks. Anna shared the inkwell with Sally Lil. Carolina got her own to use.

Anna opened her tablet to a clean page. She dipped her pen in the well.

"Hold the stylus lightly, scholars," Miss Simmons instructed as she walked around the room. "Sweep your arm gracefully."

Anna swept her arm. Her dress sleeve wiped across her letters, smudging the ink.

"Anna, how many times must I tell you to hold the pen in the right hand," Miss Simmons said. *"That* is your writing hand. Then the ink won't smudge."

Anna switched hands. The pen felt awkward, like she was holding it between her toes. She gritted her teeth. Carefully, she wrote a big *A* and a small *a,* then a big *B* and a small *b.* As she began the *C,* the pen nib stuck in a rough spot in the paper.

Frustrated, Anna pushed on the jammed point. The nib slipped and shot ink into the air, splattering the front of Carolina's pinafore.

"Miss Simmons!" she wailed. "Anna threw ink on me!"

"I did not!" Anna jumped to her feet. Her knee hit the bench and it tipped over. Tablets and inkwells crashed to the plank floor. Anna dove over the bench and caught up one inkwell before it spilled. The second one landed on top of Sally Lil's open tablet. A black stain spread across the white pages.

Sally Lil began to cry. "Papa said he can't afford another!"

Anna touched the girl's skinny shoulder. "Oh, Sally Lil, you can use mine."

"What in heaven's name is going on?" Miss Simmons bustled over. Anna didn't raise her eyes. She gulped, expecting harsh words.

"Look at my pinny!" Carolina continued to wail. "It's all Anna's fault!"

"It *was* Anna's fault, Miss Simmons," Eloise Baxter said from the recitation table. "I saw the whole thing."

"We did, too," Hattie and Ruth chimed from the stools beside her.

Tears sprang into Anna's eyes. The girls were right. It *was* her fault. Her fingers could pluck an egg from under a chicken without ruffling a feather, but she couldn't get them to manage a pen.

"I'll just leave then," Anna declared, angry at herself and the girls accusing her. "I hate all this learning anyways!" She stomped down the aisle, jerked open the door, and ran out of the school.

She raced to the rear of the building. The cold wind whipped her braid and her skirts, but she didn't care. Top was nibbling a clump of dry grass. He lifted his head and greeted her with a whinny.

"Oh, Top." Anna hugged him. "I just ain't cut out for lessons. Reading, arithmetic, penmanship. It's all too hard. Too odious."

She heard Miss Simmons call her name.

Anna buried her face in Top's mane.

Footsteps crunched closer. "There you are," the teacher said. "Come back inside before you freeze."

Anna shook her head. "No ma'am. I'm going home and herd sheep. That's a sight easier than penmanship."

"My dear Anna." Miss Simmons gently touched her arm. "I know that lessons often seem hard to you. But you've come such a long way this school year."

"But I haven't." Anna faced the teacher. Miss Simmons had thrown a woolen cloak over her shoulders. "I still can't write my ABCs. It's the same way with cross-stitch. My fingers are just too stubborn." Holding up her hands, she wiggled her fingers. "They're like a ten-mule hitch bucking at their traces."

Miss Simmons laughed. "That's a creative analogy."

"A what?"

"Anna, your mind is as sharp as this wind," Miss Simmons said, hugging her cloak tighter. "Learning just takes time. And you shouldn't listen to what the other girls say when they're being hurtful. They're just jealous because they don't have a pony as fine as yours."

"Eloise has Champ," Anna murmured as she twirled a hank of Top's mane.

"True, but I've never heard Eloise boast about

Champ herding sheep," Miss Simmons pointed out.

Anna shrugged.

"Will you please come back inside now?" Miss Simmons asked.

"We-e-l-l-l..." Anna drew out her answer. She considered going home. But if she did, Mama would probably send her right back. "If I stay, do I have to write anymore?"

Miss Simmons shook her head. "No. However, Anna, no matter what you decide, you do understand I'll have to write a note to your father and mother. You will have to buy Sally Lil a new tablet. And you may have to replace Carolina's pinafore."

Anna winced. Mama would not be pleased. Anna's family wasn't as poor as Sally Lil's. And Papa didn't have as many mouths to feed as the Freisens. But like all other homesteaders, the Vails had to be very frugal. On the prairie, money was as scarce as trees.

"I understand, ma'am," Anna said. When Mama found out about the spilled ink, she'd be mad enough to cut a switch. Anna decided she'd take her chances with Papa, who should be home about the same time school let out. "And I think I'll come back to school now."

Miss Simmons smiled. "Good. Why don't you clean

up the spilled ink while the others finish their letters? Use the old newspapers Missus Baxter gave us to use."

"Yes ma'am."

"Now let's go back inside. This wind is numbing my fingers."

Anna said goodbye to Top and Champ and hurried after the teacher.

Everyone was pretending to work when the two came into the school. But Anna could tell by their sideways glances that they'd been watching the door like hawks.

Sally Lil was seated on the bench, staring sadly at her ruined tablet. Anna gave the little girl her own to use. Then she went over to stack of newspapers piled high in the coat corner. She wadded up several sheets. While the others finished their ABCs, she wiped up the ink. This task she could well do.

"Look, Miss Simmons." Eloise held up her tablet. She'd written *How lovely is our teacher?* in perfect script.

"Very nice, Eloise," Miss Simmons said.

Anna rolled her eyes. "Teacher's pet," she muttered as she tossed the soiled newspapers into the stove.

"Everyone's work looks praiseworthy," Miss Simmons told the class. "When your ink has dried, please put your tablets away and get out your slates for arithmetic."

Anna wiped her black-stained fingers with another newspaper and then went back to her place on the bench. She sat next to Sally Lil, her slate on her knees. Miss Simmons passed out the stubby pieces of chalk. "We're running low, scholars, so bear down gently. And no chewing on the ends." She looked pointedly at William and George.

"We will be working on subtraction this day." She tapped on the blackboard with the pointer. Anna groaned. Problems covered every speck of the painted board.

"Who can tell us how we use subtraction in our lives?"

Eloise's arm shot up.

"Miss Baxter?" the teacher said. "Would you give an example, please?"

Eloise hopped to her feet. "If I have *ten* party dresses but *two* need mending, how many of my party dresses would not need mending?"

Anna snorted.

"Miss Vail? Does that ladylike noise mean you would like to answer the problem?"

Anna stood. "Yes ma'am. The answer would be *zero*

party dresses since in all my life I ain't never had one."

Beside her, Sally Lil nodded in agreement.

"And I have no earthly idea why Eloise would need ten of them," Anna added for good measure. "There ain't that many parties for her to go to. Ten *sheep* would be more practical."

"It's just an example," Eloise retorted.

"Miss Simmons, I have an example," Karl called.

The teacher sighed. "Yes, Karl. Please share your example."

"A homesteader has thirteen chickens in the coop. A coyote breaks in and kills—"

"Thank you, Karl," Miss Simmons quickly interrupted. "I think those are enough examples. William and George, please bring your slates to the recitation table. Scholars, please copy the problems on the blackboard. First Level do numbers one through five. Second Level…"

Anna got to work copying the first problem on her slate: $13-6=$___. The six came out looking like a worm, all dead and shriveled by a dry spell. "Sally Lil, can I borrow the eraser?"

Sally Lil handed Anna the block of wood wrapped in sheepskin. The little girl's fingers were icy. Anna reached around Sally Lil and tapped Carolina's shoulder. In silence the two girls switched places, Sally Lil by the stove so she could warm up, Carolina in the middle.

Anna erased the six and redrew it. This time it was as curly and smooth as a worm after a spring rain. Then she stared at the problem again. Thirteen was more than ten, she knew, but she only had ten fingers. And she couldn't see her toes. She sighed in frustration.

Miss Simmons is wrong, Anna thought. *My mind is not as sharp as the wind. It's as dull as that sooty teakettle on the stove.*

Frustrated, Anna sucked on the end of the chalk. The wind whistled through the holes around the stovepipe. A clod of dirt fell from the ceiling, plinking on top of the kettle. Steam hissed from the spout.

Anna looked up. The tip of a brown nose was sticking out from one of the holes. "Look, Sally Lil." Anna was about to show the mouse to the little girl when a long forked tongue darted from the hole.

Anna inhaled sharply. That was no mouse. It was a snake!

Goosebumps raced up Anna's arms. Clutching the slate, she watched as the snake slithered partway through the hole. She recognized the bumpy triangle-shaped head and the brown diamonds on its back.

Not just a snake. *A rattler!*

CHAPTER FOUR

M-miss Simmons," Anna croaked, fear making her throat tight.

"What now, Anna?" The teacher turned impatiently in her seat at the recitation table.

"Th-there's a rattlesnake in the ceiling."

With a scream, Miss Simmons shot off the stool, sending it crashing to the floor.

"No, no, don't move!" Anna cried out, her head tipped back, her eyes on the snake. The warning came too late. Eloise, Ruth, Hattie, and Carolina began to screech and rush around. The snake slid from the hole and wrapped itself around the stovepipe. It clung there for a moment and then fell, landing with a thud at Miss Simmons's feet.

Frozen in place, Miss Simmons screamed again. The rattler coiled, lifted its head, and shook its tail. Anna sprang from the bench. She grabbed the hot kettle off the stove. In one swift move, she poured the boiling water onto the rattler.

The snake flailed in agony. Its head struck wildly.

Anna backed out of the way. "Run! Get!" she hollered. Behind her, she heard the scurry of leather soles on the plank floor as the other children ran toward the door at the back of the school. Anna looked over just as Miss Simmons's eyes rolled back in her head and her teacher collapsed in a heap.

The rattler struck blindly at the teacher's skirts. Anna lifted the empty teakettle and brought the bottom down hard on the snake's head. Eugene ran up holding a chunk of wood. Using it like a hammer, he beat the rattler until it stopped whipping around.

Panting, Anna stood back. By now, John Jacob, William, George, and Karl were crowded around, watching the dying rattler. Its body twitched once more, then grew still.

John Jacob whistled. "Whoo-wee, Anna. Lucky you kilt that snake. It could've bitten Miss Simmons!"

"Is she all right?" Anna asked Ida. The older girl was stooped next to the teacher slapping her hand.

"She's out cold," Ida said. "Best get a cool rag on her head. Eloise, would you please dip your handkerchief in the water bucket," she called toward the back of the room, "and bring it here?"

The other girls were huddled by the door. Eloise shook her head. "No, Ida, I will *not* come up there as long as that *snake* is on the floor."

"Then at least give someone your handkerchief!" Ida said.

"I'll do it," Sally Lil offered, taking the hanky from Eloise.

Anna studied the snake. "It should be hibernating. Why do you suppose it woke up?" she asked the boys, who were still gathered around.

John Jacob shrugged. "Might be it was moving toward the heat of the stove."

"But why move now? I gather the critter's been living in the ceiling all winter."

"Might be the warmer weather woke it," Eugene suggested.

Anna glanced toward the window. It was now covered with frost. "Might be the threat of a *storm* woke it." She crouched beside the snake. "You got your knife, Eugene? I want to cut off this rattle and add it to my collection."

Just then Miss Simmons moaned.

"She's coming to," Ida said. Sally Lil hurried over

and gently set the damp handkerchief on her forehead. Anna and the boys left the snake and circled the teacher. Her long lashes fluttered. Her hand reached up to touch the cool cloth. Then her eyes opened. For a moment, she stared at them, a confused expression on her face.

"What happened?" she asked weakly.

"A rattlesnake fell from the ceiling, Miss Simmons," Ida explained.

"Don't worry, Anna whacked it with the kettle," William said.

"Then Eugene beat it," Karl chimed in.

The teacher pressed her hands to her face. "Oh *my.*"

"Don't be afraid, Miss Simmons," George said, toeing the snake with his boot. "This is just one little rattler. This summer Pa ran over a whole nest of them with his plow. Cut their heads right off."

William waved his arms excitedly. "And last winter one climbed up my bedpost! Ma had to blast it with goose shot."

"Shush! You'll frighten her worse," Ida snapped at the boys. "Anna, you and John Jacob throw that thing out of here."

Anna picked up one end, careful to grasp the snake behind the head. Its mouth gaped and she could see the fangs. John Jacob grabbed the tail. The snake was heavy and it sagged between them. As they walked toward the door, the four girls squealed and ran in the opposite direction.

John Jacob opened the door and they heaved the snake outside. It landed on the frozen ground at the bottom of the stoop. "I can cut off the rattles during recess," Anna said. "Then I'll count them. See if I can tell how old it is."

Arms wrapped around her for warmth, she gazed across the prairie. The air was moist. The sky was heavy with roiling clouds. The prairie grass rippled like a wind-whipped sheet.

"You're right about a storm coming," John Jacob said.

"I hope it snows! I want to pelt Eloise with a snow-ball." Anna made a disgusted sound. "It'd serve her right for screaming like a baby when that snake fell. She's such a sissy."

"I know." John Jacob said. "She's a *prissy* sissy."

Anna grinned at him, hoping they were friends again. But before she could say anything else he muttered, "I wonder how Miss Simmons is getting along," and hurried inside.

Anna trudged in after him.

In front of the room Ida and Ruth were helping Miss Simmons over to her desk chair. Eugene stood awkwardly, his big hands clasped behind him as if afraid to touch her. Ida had hold of the teacher's left elbow. Ruth was guiding from the right. Hattie and Carolina darted behind, stepping on her skirts and getting in the way.

Eloise sat on the second bench, as pale-faced as Miss Simmons. "Wait until my father hears about this near tragedy!" she said loudly. No one paid her any mind. Rattlesnakes were deadly, but all too common on the prairie.

The younger boys were busily counting at the recitation table. Karl was stoking the stove. Anna sat next to Sally Lil. "I filled the tea kettle again," she told Anna. "Eugene helped me put it on the stove. We'll need the water for washing up at lunchtime."

"Thank you, Sally Lil. You were a good help."

Sally Lil smiled shyly. "And you were brave, Anna."

"Thank you, scholars," Miss Simmons announced shakily. She was seated at her desk, Eloise's damp handkerchief pressed to her forehead. "I feel much better. And I apologize to you all."

"There ain't no rattlers in Boston?" Karl asked her.

"Not that I know of, Karl. Now, let's get back to our subtraction lessons."

Anna let out a groan. Neither a snake nor fainting could keep Miss Simmons from arithmetic. "She sure is persistent about learning," she whispered to Sally Lil.

Once again, Anna picked up her slate. Despite all the excitement, 13-6=＿＿＿ was still written on it.

"Unless I grow more fingers, I'll never figure this out. Sally Lil, lemme borrow a hand."

Using Sally Lil's hand, Anna found enough fingers to solve the problem. She wrote down the answer and then looked back up to the blackboard. Her jaw dropped. Was it her imagination or were there more problems on it?

"Seems like numbers are sprouting faster than summer weeds," she grumbled.

She propped her chin on her hand. Her mind strayed outside to the brisk wind and the heavy clouds. *I better check on Top,* she thought. She wanted to make sure he was still tied—as well as get out of ciphering.

Setting her slate and chalk under the bench, she raised her arm. When Miss Simmons looked her way, she held up two fingers, the signal to use the privy. The teacher nodded.

Anna jumped up, hurried to the corner, and pulled her jacket off the hook. She slipped it on as she walked to the door.

Karl looked at her over his shoulder. "Don't let that rattler back in," he joked.

Anna cracked open the door and slid into the icy wind. Holding her jacket closed, she leaped off the stoop and over the snake. She raced around the corner of the school and past the lean-to. Top and Champ stood side by side behind the schoolhouse, their rumps toward the wind. Their heads were down; their tails were tucked.

"Top, you all right?" Anna asked. She rubbed her hand down the pony's soft face. "We had an unwanted visitor, and I almost forgot you in all the excitement."

He nudged her jacket pocket.

"No apple until lunchtime." She hugged his fuzzy neck. "Won't be long though."

She moved Top's stake closer to the back of the school, so he'd be sheltered from the wind. She had to leave Champ tied to the tree. "Sorry," she told him. "Maybe Eloise will think to care for you," she added, although she knew it wouldn't happen.

Then Anna ran to the not-so-nice. A gust threatened to blow the door from her grasp, and she struggled to shut it behind her.

Once it was latched, she pulled down her woolen drawers. She braced herself against the cold and sat over the hole in the wooden seat. An old copy of *Frank Leslie's Boys' and Girls' Weekly* lay on the floor. The cover showed a lady riding sidesaddle. She wore a plumed hat and held a whip in one hand. With the other hand, she yanked hard on the reins of the rearing horse.

Anna snorted. *That lady rides like Eloise,* she thought, *with stiff arms and fingers.* Anna knew that a horse needed a gentle touch. No wonder the one in the magazine was trying to throw his rider.

She leafed through the curled and musty pages, looking for more horse pictures. A dead spider on the floor caught her attention. She picked it up and studied the dried body and crumpled legs. Eloise hated spiders. Grinning, Anna tucked it carefully in her jacket pocket.

She swung her feet, wondering how long she could sit out here without anyone noticing. Maybe she'd miss the entire arithmetic lesson.

Suddenly a mighty gust rocked the privy. Frigid air blasted up through the hole, chilling her bare bottom.

Anna ripped out a page from the magazine, finished up, and tugged on her stockings.

She opened the privy door and peeked out. She gasped. The clouds *had* brought snow! Papa might cuss it. And Mama might dread it. But Anna loved snow. It meant sledding, skating, snow forts, and, if deep enough, *no school!*

Anna shut the door and latched it behind her. Sticking out her tongue, she caught a flake. Then she twirled across the schoolyard until her hair was damp and her head swam dizzily. When she reached the schoolhouse door, she flung it open and shouted, "Guess what, everybody? It's snowing!"

CHAPTER FIVE

Snow!" John Jacob leaped off the bench and joined Anna on the stoop.

"Bully," said Karl. "It's snowing like topsy!"

The three of them took turns swinging each other by the elbows until Anna was breathless.

Miss Simmons bustled to the doorway. "Children, stop!" She stamped her foot. "Come inside this instant. Lessons are *not* over."

John Jacob's face grew red. "I'm sorry, Miss Simmons," he apologized as he darted past her into the building.

"Me too," Karl mumbled, following him.

Anna sighed and hurried into the schoolhouse.

Eugene was by the door shrugging into his coat. "I need to get the cows in," he told Miss Simmons.

"What about lessons, Eugene?" she asked, but he was already striding out of the classroom.

"His papa is sickly and his mama counts on him," Anna explained.

"Yes, yes, I know." Turning, the teacher clapped her hands sharply. "Now, let's get back to arithmetic."

William, George, and Sally Lil were over by the window, pushing to catch a glimpse outside. At the sound of the clap, they scurried to their seats.

"You'd think you children had never seen snow before," Miss Simmons said.

Anna hung up her jacket. Reaching in her pocket, she gently plucked out the spider. Slowly she walked behind the row of girls on the second bench.

She stopped behind Eloise. "Champ is fine," she whispered as she dropped the spider onto her puffy velvet sleeve. "In case you wanted to know."

"I *didn't*," Eloise replied haughtily. "He's just an *animal.*"

Anna had no reply for such a foolish remark. She slid onto the front bench. Carolina was next to the warm stove, a shawl over her shoulders. Sally Lil was in the middle. She was shivering and her lips were blue. "You smell like a horse," she whispered to Anna.

"Top would be pleased." Anna looked closer at the little girl. "Sally Lil, don't you have a coat?"

The little girl flushed pink. "It was so sunny today that Ma said I didn't need to wear it."

Anna frowned. Now that she thought back, Sally Lil was always absent on really cold days. She guessed that meant she had no coat. Or it was so raggedy she was too ashamed to wear it.

"Then you need to sit next to the stove again. Carolina," Anna hissed, "you've got a shawl. Let Sally Lil by the stove."

Carolina gave her a snooty look. "No, Anna, I will not. It's my turn by the stove."

"Ladies, what is the problem now?" Miss Simmons demanded. She was again seated at the recitation table, helping William and George count using the abacus.

Anna stood up. "It's actually my turn at the stove, Miss Simmons, and I give it to Sally Lil."

"Thank you, Anna. That's kind of you. Now please sit down and finish your subtraction drill or we'll never complete our studies."

Carolina stomped to the far end of the bench. Sally Lil scooted over toward the stove. Anna settled next to her, her slate on her legs. Carefully she wrote the second problem, 14-7=_____. She gnawed on the end of her braid.

Raising her arm, she held up three fingers, the signal for a drink. Miss Simmons nodded but her face looked pinched. Anna slid the slate under her seat and walked back to the water bucket. It stood behind the second bench on the boys' side. She stooped beside the bucket. Taking her time, she dunked the dipper into the water, breaking through a film of ice that had formed on top. She raised the dipper to her lips. She sipped daintily.

"Delicious." She smacked her lips as if it was fine cider.

John Jacob turned slightly in his seat. "Think it'll be a big 'un?" he whispered.

Anna nodded. "Enough to bury the school. Then we won't have school tomorrow!" She took another sip.

"I'd rather not miss Miss Simmons's lessons." John Jacob shook his head sadly.

The sip slid the wrong way down Anna's throat. She coughed hard, spilling water from the dipper across the floor.

"Anna?" Miss Simmons called toward the back.

"I'm all right, Miss Simmons," she choked out. Grabbing the hem of her skirt, she wiped up the floor. When she hurried back to her seat, she glanced at Eloise. The spider still jiggled on her puffy sleeve.

Anna was just reaching for her slate when a scream pierced the room.

"Get it off! Get it off!"

Anna spun around. Eloise was hopping furiously up and down. Her head was twisted awkwardly. Her right shoulder was cocked.

"Get what off?" Hattie cried. Lifting her legs, she stared fearfully at the floor. "Is it another snake?"

Ruth scrambled onto the bench. "Snake!"

"No! A spider! A spider's on my shoulder," Eloise screeched.

Ida grabbed Eloise, who was twirling like a top. "Hold still." She gripped Eloise's arm and flicked the spider from her sleeve. "It's dead. So *hush.*"

"Why, it must have dropped from the ceiling," Anna said, straight-faced.

"Just like the snake," Sally Lil exclaimed and all eyes looked upward.

"Enough!" Miss Simmons whacked the tabletop with her pointer. "Scholars, put away your slates. We will break for recess and lunch—"

Karl whooped. Anna let out a yee-haw.

Rap, rap, rap! Miss Simmons banged furiously. "Sit down. We will pass in an orderly fashion," she shouted above the cheering and chattering.

The noise slowly died and everyone settled back on the benches.

Miss Simmons exhaled loudly. "Thank you. John Jacob, you are responsible for the wash water and soap. You may pass."

John Jacob rose and lifted the teakettle from the stove.

"Second bench, girls. Stand, turn, and pass for lunch and recess."

Eloise, Hattie, Ruth, and Ida walked single file to the coat corner. Anna wiggled impatiently on the bench. Recess was her favorite part of the school day, and it was even better when it was snowing! She glanced at Miss Simmons, slightly ashamed for disrupting arithmetic, but not ashamed enough to let it dampen her high spirits.

When the girls on the first bench were dismissed, Anna strode to the coat corner. Eloise was still there, slowly sliding on her kid gloves. "I know it was you, Anna."

Anna tried to look shocked. "It wasn't."

"It *was*," Eloise insisted. "You're the only one *mean* enough." With a toss of her long hair and scarf, she flounced out the door.

"It was you, Anna," Sally Lil repeated matter of factly. "I saw you drop the spider."

Anna gave her a wink, then washed her hands in the

bucket on the floor and dried them on the rag. She pulled her jacket off the hook. "Here, Sally Lil. You wear this jacket outside." She plucked her cap, glove, and wristlets from the pockets. "I've got on woolen underdrawers."

The little girl's face lit up. "Thank you," she said as she took the jacket.

Anna put on her cap and retrieved her lunch pail. When she stepped outside, mushy flakes plopped on her nose. Already an inch of snow coated the ground.

"Woo hoo!" She leaped off the stoop.

William and George were staring down at the snow-covered snake, which now looked like a loopy white rope. William was munching a bacon sandwich.

"Can we kick it?" George asked Anna as if the carcass belonged to her.

"Sure. But I claim the rattles."

George nodded and took a big bite of his boiled egg.

Anna and Sally Lil joined Karl and John Jacob, who were leaning against the side wall of the school eating. Both boys were telling snake stories. They talked at the same time, their mouths full.

"Last spring Ida shot one off the roof," John Jacob said. "Put a big hole in the sod."

"That ain't nothin'. Ma found one curled in the pigs'

slop bucket." Karl chuckled. "I ain't never seen a lady run so fast!"

"Where's Ida and the others?" Anna asked.

"Ida stayed in to help Miss Simmons." John Jacob nodded toward the lean-to. "The others are huddled in there having a tea party."

"So they can wear all those *party* dresses," Karl said, and the two boys sniggered.

Anna sat in a windswept bare spot and lifted the lid of her lunch pail. Sally Lil sat beside her, so close their shoulders touched. Sally Lil had brought a shriveled baked potato in an old tobacco tin. John Jacob pulled a lard sandwich wrapped in brown paper from his pocket.

There were several cold biscuits in Anna's pail. She passed one to Sally Lil and one to John Jacob. They accepted them silently. Mama always packed extras, knowing well that other families had less food and more mouths.

Anna bit into her baked sweet potato. It was crumbly and earthy-tasting. Mama had also packed her favorite, a gooseberry tart, as well as a handful of dried apple slices. Anna shared the apples, too, keeping back two slices for the horses.

"We should make some snowballs and sneak up on the girls," John Jacob said.

Karl scooped up a handful. "It ain't packing yet. Too wet."

"That'd be mean to hit the girls," Sally Lil declared. "Anna was already mean to Eloise."

John Jacob's jaw dropped. "*You* put that spider on her shoulder?"

Anna shrugged. "Weren't nothing."

Karl and John Jacob burst into hearty guffaws. "Were too! She was twirling around so fast, we could see her lace-trimmed petticoats!"

Sally Lil sighed. "I wish I had lace-trimmed petticoats."

"Not me," Anna said. "You can't ride a horse with frills bunched up around your knees."

"You can ride sidesaddle, like Eloise," Sally Lil said.

Karl leaned closer. "When Miss Simmons toppled over, I saw *her*—"

John Jacob punched him hard on the arm.

"Ow!" Karl rubbed his sleeve. "What was that for?"

"I won't have you saying anything disrespectful about Miss Simmons," John Jacobs said gruffly.

Anna stopped in mid-chew and stared at John Jacob. Her friend's face was tight and red.

"By golly," Karl said in amazement. "You *are* sweet on Miss Simmons."

"I am not." John Jacob shoved the last of his brown

bread in his mouth and scrambled to his feet.

"Where are you going?" Anna asked.

"To take some wood in. If it keeps snowing, we're going to need it."

He strode off around the corner. Karl shrugged and said, "Sure acts like he's sweet on her."

"Oh hush," Anna said grumpily. She gave Sally Lil the rest of her gooseberry tart and stepped away from the wall. "I'm going to check on Top."

Anna trotted to the back of the schoolhouse. The wind stung her ears and flapped her skirt around her calves. She tugged her knit hat lower. The flakes were falling faster.

Top whinnied when he saw her. He'd stomped the snow and grass into a muddy circle. "Are you fretting about the weather?" she asked as she patted him on the neck.

Champ was still tied directly in the path of the wind. Snow covered his rump and icicles hung from his long mane. Anna doubted that Eloise had checked on him once.

Anna hurried over to him. "Eloise doesn't care a whit for you," she said, tugging an icicle from his forelock. "If I owned a horse as fine as you, I'd treat you like a prince."

Untying his reins, she led him closer to the back wall of the school and tied him loosely to a post. Then she used her sleeve to brush the snow off his back.

"That's better." She fed Top one apple slice and Champ the other. "Now you two be nice to each other." Anna gave Top a stern look, but for once her pony wasn't pinning his ears at the bigger horse.

She marched around to the front of the schoolhouse, looking back at the prints her boots made in the snow. It wasn't deep enough to make a fort, but it was getting just right for snowballs.

Karl was sucking on a piece of taffy. Sally Lil was licking the last of the gooseberry tart from her purple-stained fingers.

"Karl," Anna called. She bent over and scraped up a handful of snow. "Let's get John Jacob and attack that lean-to."

They found John Jacob heading into the school with an armful of wood. "I can't yet. Gotta get this wood inside."

"Teacher's pet," Karl taunted.

As soon as they began making snowballs, William and George joined them. The flakes were growing smaller as the air got colder. Anna gazed across the prairie, now a woolly white blanket.

"We'll surround the lean-to and start throwing on the count of four," Karl said when they had a pile of snowballs. "I'll signal with my fingers."

"Who made you the general?" William asked.

Karl propped his fists on his hips. "My grandpa fought in the Civil War!" he declared. "So I know a thing or two about soldiering."

"You can both be generals," Anna said. "Now let's commence this battle before Miss Simmons rings the bell."

Minutes later, a snowball in each hand, they sneaked toward the lean-to. The boys tiptoed around the right side. Anna and Sally Lil went to the left. When they got close, Anna held a finger to her lips and listened.

Eloise was talking about her oldest sister, Imogene, who had a beau named Henry.

"Did you really see her kiss Henry in the parlor?" Ruth asked.

"Ooh-la-la, *yes*." Eloise started to giggle.

On the other side of the lean-to, Karl waved to catch Anna's attention. He held up one finger, then two as he mouthed, "One...two..."

Anna drew back her throwing arm.

Karl held up a third finger. "Three!"

Suddenly an eerie moan filled the air. At the same instant a gust of icy snow whirled like a tornado from the sky. The blast hit Anna full force and she staggered backward.

Then she heard the screech of metal tearing from wood as the wind ripped a board off the slanted side of the lean-to and sent it flying right into Sally Lil!

Chapter Six

The board hit Sally Lil square in the chest, knocking her to the ground. Hattie, Ruth, Eloise, and Carolina shot from under the lean-to. Screeching as loudly as the ripped metal, they scattered across the schoolyard like fox-chased chickens.

Anna squatted next to Sally Lil. The little girl was sprawled flat on her back in the snow. Tears coursed down her pale cheeks and she clutched her skinny chest.

"Oh, Sally Lil! Are you hurt?" Anna exclaimed.

The boys huddled around her. William began crying, too. "She's going to die," he sobbed.

Sally Lil shook her head. "I ain't going to die," she whispered, her lips barely moving.

"What's wrong? Where does it hurt?" Anna squeezed the little girl's arm, hunting for wounds.

"Should we get Doc Knowles?" Karl asked.

Sally Lil shook her head again. "No. Nothing's busted."

Anna frowned. "Then what's wrong?"

Slowly, Sally Lil sat up. Hands trembling, she unbuttoned Anna's jacket. A biscuit was smashed against the bib of her pinafore.

"I was saving it for my little sister, Jenny Sue," Sally Lil snuffled. "We ain't had biscuits made with milk and eggs since fall. Now it's ruin't!"

The boys began to chortle with relief. Anna heaved a sigh. "Oh, Sally Lil. Tomorrow I'll bring you and Jenny Sue a whole basket of biscuits."

Her eyes lit up. "You will?"

William was inspecting the roof of the lean-to. "This'll need fixing," he said. He scanned the horizon. "Wind swept that board clean to the next county."

Sally Lil rose unsteadily to her feet. Anna helped her brush the snow off her skirt and stockings. Miss Simmons rang the bell. William, Karl, and George quickly tossed their snowballs at the ruined lean-to. "Bulls eye!" they hollered as they threw. "Gotcha!"

The bell rang again. Anna and Sally Lil followed the boys into the school. As she walked, Sally Lil picked biscuit crumbs from her pinafore. "Ain't wasting a lick," she said as she popped them in her mouth.

Miss Simmons was waiting at the door. "Sally Lil? Are you all right?" she asked anxiously. "Karl just told me that a board blew off the lean-to and hit you."

"Yes ma'am, it did. But I'll be right as rain soon as I finish eatin' what's left of this biscuit."

"I'm glad to hear you're not hurt." Miss Simmons peered out the open door. "The girls said the wind's picking up."

"Yes'm," Anna replied. She pulled off her cap, which was frosted white. "It's nearing a squall."

"Perhaps it will die down before dismissal. There are some rags in the cloak corner. You and Sally Lil dry off."

Anna stamped the snow off her boots. The warmth inside the schoolhouse made her fingers tingle. As she wiped her damp cheeks, she wondered if Miss Simmons would dismiss school early.

The other children had placed their soggy mittens, hats, and gloves on the floor near the stove. Then they'd pushed the benches closer to the heat, trying to dry their wet boots, stockings, and pant legs. Anna sat down next to Sally Lil.

Karl waved his hand.

"Yes, Karl?" Miss Simmons said from beside her desk.

"Will you dismiss us early?"

"Let's wait and see if the snow will blow over," Miss Simmons replied. "It seems many of your Nebraska storms end as soon as they begin. If it gets worse, perhaps your fathers will fetch you." She held up a book. "We'll have some quiet time while I read from *Hans Brinker or The Silver Skates.*"

The children cheered. Even Anna loved story reading. *The Silver Skates* wasn't as thrilling as Buffalo Bill, but Hans and his sister Gretel and their friends were similar to Anna and her friends.

Hans's father was sick like Eugene's father. Gretel dreaded books like Anna. Hans wore patched clothes like Sally Lil. Hilda van Gleck, the rich burgomaster's daughter, wore rich furs and velvet like Eloise. And Voostenwalbert Schimmelpenninck, the small boy with the big name, reminded her of William, whose last name was also much too long for Anna to pronounce.

Anna settled on the bench, Sally Lil leaning cozily against her side. She listened raptly as Miss Simmons began to read.

"Beautiful Katrinka! Flushed with youth and health, all life and mirth and motion."

Who at school is like Katrinka? Anna wondered. Certainly not *she.*

Katrinka was a "pretty little maiden" with golden

hair that streamed in the sunlight. And more importantly, she could skate faster than anyone. *And of course,* Anna thought dreamily, *Katrinka is bound to win those silver skates!*

Anna sighed, wishing she was like Katrinka. The last time she'd skated on the river, she'd spent most of the time on her bottom.

Anna grew drowsy, only half hearing as Miss Simmons finished reading the end of the chapter.

"What wonder that it seemed his darkest hour when, years afterward, thy presence floated away from him forever." Miss Simmons clapped the book shut, making Anna jump. "Tomorrow," said the teacher, "we'll read chapter four."

"Awww, Miss Simmons. Can't you read more?" George asked. The others joined in the chorus.

"How about *The Legend of Sleepy Holler?*" Karl suggested. "You read that before Christmas. It was right spooky!"

Miss Simmons laughed. "It's *The Legend of Sleepy Holl*-ow," she corrected.

"Oh, Miss Simmons, I didn't like that story," Eloise said. "It's too scary."

"Yes, Washington Irving did write a hair-raising tale."

"I bet that Brom Bones would fall in love with *you,* Miss Simmons," Sally Lil said wistfully.

"No, he wouldn't!" John Jacob jumped up, his fingers curled into fists. Anna and the others stared at him. Flushing pink, he sat down.

"Well." Miss Simmons cleared her throat and opened *Hans Brinker* again. "I suppose we have time to begin chapter four."

Bump. A noise outside the schoolhouse door startled Anna. Miss Simmons looked up from her open book. Sally Lil blinked sleepily. "What was that?" she whispered to Anna.

Thump, bang.

Anna twisted on the bench. All heads turned and stared at the closed door. Had Eloise's father arrived with his buggy? He'd often show up unannounced during school hours. Sometimes he'd walk around the room, peering over shoulders. Or he'd sit on the back bench, a pad in his hand, watching Miss Simmons teach. Other times he'd pick up Eloise early because it was raining, or a relation was visiting, or the seamstress needed her for a fitting.

Thump, thump, thump, thumpety-thump. Anna swallowed. This caller didn't sound like Mister Baxter.

Miss Simmons slowly closed the book. One hand

went to her throat. "Why, who could be making that racket?" she asked.

Bam! The door shook and the latch rattled as if someone had hit it hard.

"Someone's trying to break in," Carolina gasped.

Sally Lil clutched Anna's arm. Eloise, Hattie, and Ruth scooted tightly together on the bench. John Jacob and Karl faced the door.

Bang! Anna jumped from her seat, too scared to stay still.

"Too bad Eugene ain't here," Karl whispered.

Miss Simmons smiled bravely. "I better go see who our impatient caller could be," she said. Setting the book on her desk, she picked up the pointer. As she walked down the aisle, she held it in front of her like a club.

Ida rose to her feet. "I'll go with you."

"Me too." Anna hurried around the bench and joined them. John Jacob grabbed a chunk of wood and Karl picked up his lunch pail. Together they approached the door.

Bang, crack!

The door rattled so violently the small group froze before it.

Outside, Anna could hear the whine of the wind and

the snow pelting against the door. "It's the storm," she whispered. "It's trying to batter its way inside."

Thumpety, thumpety, BANG!

Suddenly the latch rattled free and the door flew open. Anna gasped. There on the stoop stood a snow-covered beast!

A powerful gust of wind whipped into the school. Ida and Miss Simmons were swept backwards. John Jacob dropped the chunk of wood.

The beast reared its shaggy white head.

"Run!" Karl hollered.

CHAPTER SEVEN

Top!" Anna yelled, and rushed toward the icy monster. "It's Top Hat!" Anna hollered above the wind. The pony clattered into the schoolroom, toppling a pile of wood and kicking over an empty lunch pail. He shook his mane, spraying ice everywhere.

"Oh, Top, you're a snow horse!" Anna grabbed a rag from the corner and began to wipe him off. Behind her, the door hung open and sheets of snow blew inside. John Jacob tried to push it shut. It was then that Anna noticed that Top was dragging his rope, the stake hanging from the end.

Miss Simmons bustled over. "Karl, help John Jacob with that the door," she instructed. "We can't have it flying off the hinges. Anna, your pony cannot stay in here."

"He must have pulled out his stake." Anna held up the rope. "He's never done that before."

"No matter. He *can't* stay in here. Boys, get ready to open the door so Anna can lead her pony outside."

"But it's too cold," Anna protested. "He might freeze!"

Miss Simmons gave Anna a firm look. "I'm sorry. I cannot have a pony disrupting my class. Snakes, spiders, why we've had enough scares already! Surely there's a spot you can tie him close by where he'll be sheltered. Perhaps by the lean-to."

Anna's shoulders slumped. "I guess."

Miss Simmons's gaze softened. "I don't know much about horses, Anna. But I do know they grow a thick winter coat."

"Yes ma'am," Anna said. "But may I please finish wiping him off first?"

"Yes, but use newspaper. We may need the rags for ourselves. And after you secure him, please wipe up the doorway."

"Yes'm."

"Now, the rest of you, let's get settled again for story reading."

Anna took her time brushing the snow off Top. The pony stood quietly behind the boy's bench. His ears were pricked as if listening to Miss Simmons read about Hans, Gretel, and the lovely Katrinka.

Finally, Anna put on her cap, gloves, and jacket. She wound a scarf around her neck and turned Top toward the door. John Jacob opened it for her. The wind was blowing so hard, he had to strain to keep the door from tearing from his grasp. Ducking her chin, Anna led Top onto the stoop. The door closed behind them with a *thunk.*

The cold instantly pierced her jacket. Snow pattered against her forehead and cheeks. Anna peered across the schoolyard. She wiped snow from her lashes, and looked again. The prairie had disappeared!

The snow was so thick and the wind so fierce that Anna couldn't see a foot in front of her. She had heard about storms like this. Some folks called them white-outs. Papa called them blizzards. No matter what their names, they could be deadly.

Top butted her nervously. Anna drew in a shaky breath, and the frosty air burned her throat. She turned left. She needed to find Champ and move both horses in front of the lean-to, which would afford some shelter.

Keeping her shoulder to the sod wall, she felt her way to the corner. Slowly, one hand on the wall and the other on Top's mane, she inched along the side. She stopped in front of the window, now a frosty, golden square. She rubbed a spot in the frost with her fist. Sally Lil's nose was pressed to the glass. When she saw Anna, she waved.

Anna wiggled stiff fingers and then trudged to the back of the school. A snowdrift angled up the rear wall where Top had been staked.

"Champ! Champ!" Anna shouted, but the wind whisked her cries into the blowing snow. There was no sign of him. Then she saw fresh tracks leading away from the school in the direction of the Baxters' farm. The snow wasn't too deep for a big horse like Champ. She hoped he would make it safely down the lane to the barn.

"Come on, Top," she mumbled behind her scarf. "Wind's too strong back here." Turning, she retraced their tracks, which were quickly vanishing. As she passed the window, a blast of wind blew her off her feet and into a drift. Snow filled her eyes and mouth.

She spit, coughed. Grasping the lead line, she pulled herself up and stood against Top, quivering. The snow surged around them in a whirlwind of white. Through the gloves, her fingers grew sharp with pain. Anna looked right, then left. She couldn't see the school!

She was trembling from head to toe. She took a deep breath, trying to shake off the panic. *Think, Anna, think.* Holding tightly to Top, she thrust out one arm. When her hand hit sod, relief filled her. Hurrying now, she made her way to the corner. Her boots were sodden, her toes numb. She stumbled against the edge of the stoop. The door flung wide.

"Anna!" Arms dragged her inside. She held tightly to the pony's rope. "Top too!" she mumbled between frozen lips.

"Yes, of course." Miss Simmons shrugged out of her long cloak and wrapped it around Anna. Ida began unlacing Anna's boots. Sally Lil held Anna's hands between hers. Karl shut the door, and he and John Jacob used the broom to sweep the snow off Top.

"Sally Lil was watching from the window," Miss Simmons said. "She saw you fall and *disappear.* Oh, I had no idea the storm had gotten so violent or I never would have sent you and Top outside. I was starting out to find you. Thank heavens you're all right."

"Ain't a storm no more," John Jacob said solemnly. "It's a blizzard."

"A blizzard?" Miss Simmons repeated as she buttoned the cloak around Anna. "That sounds ominous."

John Jacob nodded. "I don't know what ominous

means, but if it's real bad, I expect it might describe a blizzard."

Anna's teeth clacked together.

"Ominous means unfavorable, threatening," Miss Simmons said brightly as if her cheeriness would ease the unpleasant words.

Ida pulled off Anna's boots. "Her stockings are soaked through, Miss Simmons."

"Come, Anna, let's get you over to the stove." Miss Simmons steered her down the aisle.

Anna glanced over her shoulder at Top, who was receiving much attention from the boys. Carolina scooted over on the bench, making room on the end closest to the stove. Anna rubbed her half-frozen feet and wiggled her toes.

"We'd best prepare for dismissal," Miss Simmons said.

Hattie raised her arm. "Miss Simmons, Ruth and I ain't allowed to go outside in a whiteout."

"A whiteout?" Miss Simmons repeated.

"That's when it's snowing so hard you can't see," Karl explained. "Like it's doing now."

William jumped to his feet. "My Uncle Billy got lost in a whiteout," he announced. "Froze to death right outside the barn door."

George nodded. "Last year during a whiteout some of our cattle wandered onto the river. They fell through the ice and drowned."

"In that same storm Pa found three sheep frozen solid," John Jacob added.

Anna shivered and clutched the cloak tightly around her. Were *her* sheep safe? Had Little Seth and Mama thought to get them in from the field? And was her family safe? Had Papa made it back from town? Now that the weather had changed from snow flurries to a blizzard, a passel of worries raced through her mind. She shivered again, even though the stove was slowly warming her.

"During the last storm, my brother had to find shelter in a haystack," Ruth said. "He was so frostbit that he lost the tips of his toes and fingers."

"That ain't nothin'," Karl said. "Our neighbor Mister Alvie's feet was so frostbit they had to be cut off!"

Miss Simmons's face turned chalk-white. "These stories are *true?*"

"Yes'm, Miss Simmons, the stories are true," Ida said in her calm way. "It would be folly to dismiss us in the middle of a blizzard."

"But I wanna go home!" Carolina wailed.

"Well, then, perhaps your parents will come get you all," Miss Simmons said hopefully. "John Jacob and Ida, your farm is just down the way."

John Jacob shook his head. "If Pa was coming, he would've been here by now. I'm afraid the blizzard's too fierce even for him."

"My pa will come," Eloise said, her lower lip trembling. "He'll hitch the team to the sled. Nothing will stop him."

"There!" Miss Simmons clapped her hands. "Eloise's father can take us in turns to the Baxters' house until the blizzard blows over."

"Can we play with your store-bought dolls, Eloise?" Ruth asked. "The ones with real hair?"

"Will Imogene and her beau be there?" Hattie asked.

"Will your Mama make us hot cocoa?" Carolina chimed in. "I'm thirsty."

"I'm hungry," Sally Lil said.

Anna shot a look at John Jacob. He was picking at a dirty fingernail. They caught each other's eye. He frowned and shook his head. She knew what he was thinking. *No one, not even Mister Baxter, could make it through a whiteout.*

"E-E-loise, I b-believe Champ headed home," Anna

said between chattering teeth.

Eloise brightened. "There then. My parents will see him and immediately send help."

The younger kids again began talking excitedly about staying at the Baxters'.

"Miss Simmons," Ida spoke above their chatter. "Mister Baxter may not be able to make it through the storm. There's a good chance we'll be here for the night."

"For the night?" Miss Simmons repeated, her voice rising. "But we have no food. No beds. No quilts. How will we manage?"

"We have wood and water," Ida said. "That will get us through."

"No, no, we *can't* stay here all night." Miss Simmons began striding back and forth in front of the blackboard. She rubbed her upper arms nervously. "It *will* stop snowing, Ida. You'll see."

"But what if it doesn't?" Carolina whined.

Anna glanced around. All eyes were on Miss Simmons, waiting for her to reply with wise and comforting words. But the teacher kept pacing and rubbing, pacing and rubbing.

She's too frightened to speak, Anna thought. *Surely there's some way we can help.* She jumped from the bench. "I know! Let's pretend we're pioneers. Like Lewis and Clark. Or Daniel Boone. They didn't fret over snow."

"A bully idea," said John Jacob. "I can pretend I'm Grandpapa Friesen. He went out West to pan gold and got caught in an avalanche."

"We can pitch a tent," George suggested.

William snorted. "We ain't got no canvas or poles, silly."

"I am not silly," George retorted and the two started tussling.

"I've a book on Lewis and Clark." Eloise said. "I brought it from home. I can read a passage."

"Oh, do, Eloise, do," Hattie and Ruth begged.

Miss Simmons stopped pacing. She managed a wan smile. "I think that's an excellent idea, Eloise. And while you're reading, Anna and Ida will help me go through the lunch pails. We'll see if there is any food left."

Anna rose and draped Miss Simmons's cloak on the back of her desk chair. Then she checked on Top. He was eating stray bits of dried grass poking from the sod. Frost was forming on the inside walls, causing the newspapers to curl up. Anna looked at the wood and cow chips piled by the stove. There appeared to be plenty. But she knew well that a stove in winter had the appetite of a hungry bear.

She patted Top. Already his furry coat was drying. Then she joined Ida and Miss Simmons in the corner. "We need to keep the fire stoked," Anna told her teacher. "Though if it gets any colder, the wood might not last all night."

"Oh, we won't be here all night," Miss Simmons said confidently as she and Ida gathered tins and pails. "Didn't you hear Eloise? Her father will rescue us. Soon we'll be in the Baxters' parlor sipping hot cocoa."

Abruptly, Ida rose to her full height. She thrust out her chin, and there was a steely glint in her eyes. Anna recognized that look. It usually meant that one of the little Friesens was going to get a switching.

"Miss Simmons," Ida declared. "I didn't want to say it in front of the little ones, but Mister Baxter will not be rescuing us tonight. No one will get through until it stops snowing. Until the storm dies down, we are stuck here, and *we must make do!*"

CHAPTER EIGHT

Miss Simmons's face went ashy gray, and Anna wondered if she was going to faint again. But then the teacher turned away and began gathering up the lunch pails.

"Boys! Stop that!" Ida hurried to the front of the room to break up another squabble between William and George.

Anna was lifting the lid off a pail when a muffled sob caught her attention. She peered sideways. Miss Simmons was crying. Tears dripped down her cheeks, plinking like raindrops on the lid of a lunch pail.

Miss Simmons isn't much older than Ida, Anna realized. *And she's from a fancy city where they don't have rattlers or whiteouts. No wonder she's scared out of her wits.*

Suddenly Anna felt sorry for the school ma'am from back East. Anna and most of her classmates had lived through blizzards before so it wasn't quite as frightening to them.

Gently she touched the teacher's sleeve. "Maybe we *won't* be snowbound, Miss Simmons," she said quietly.

"I surely do hope you're right, Anna," Miss Simmons whispered.

Ida bustled back. "The room is getting chilled," she said. "We mustn't let the fire die down. We have to keep the little ones warm."

Miss Simmons nodded. Then she took a shuddering breath. When she finally turned toward Ida, her eyes were clear. "Yes, you're right. Thank you, Ida."

"We could bring in the rest of the wood and the cow chips from the lean-to," Anna suggested, "before the snow gets too deep."

"No, no." Miss Simmons shook her head. "I can't send someone outside in this weather. Not after hearing those horrid tales!"

"Did you find any food to share?" Ida asked.

"A boiled egg, two pieces of taffy, a chaw of jerked meat, and a handful of dried plums," Anna recited as she picked through the tins.

"I found a baked potato, half a jam sandwich, a biscuit, and three pickles," Miss Simmons said. "Why that's almost a feast!" she added with forced gaiety.

Ida frowned. "It'll have to do. At least we can melt snow for water. I'll check to make sure the kettle is full."

Anna put the lids back on the pails. As she worked, she chewed on the tip of her braid. She could hear the wind raging outside. She placed her palm on the wall in front of her. The sod blocks were freezing despite the heat from the stove. She looked up at the ceiling. Unless they kept the stove going, snow would build up on the roof. She'd heard tales of roofs collapsing from the weight.

The need for wood, for *heat,* was great, Anna knew. She pictured the lean-to. It was only about twenty yards from the front stoop. Could one person get to it and back safely?

A grand idea came to her. She ran over to John Jacob. He was stretched on the bench, his eyes closed, as he and the others listened to Eloise read from her book.

"John Jacob!" she whispered in his ear, startling him.

"W-wha—?" He flailed his arms, lost his balance, and rolled off the bench onto the floor.

"Excuse me, Anna, but I am trying to read," Eloise huffed.

"Sorry." Anna stooped beside John Jacob. "I didn't mean to scare you."

"I weren't scared," he grumbled as he picked himself up. Brushing off his pants, he sat back on the bench.

Anna sat next to him. "Are you ready for an adventure?" she whispered.

He cocked one brow. "What'd you have in mind?"

"We need to get the rest of the wood from the lean-to."

"Oh, no." He held up his hands. "I ain't losing my fingers and toes."

"Why, I thought you'd be excited," Anna said, disappointed. "We've always had adventures." Ever since John Jacob had gone sweet on the teacher, he'd changed.

"Going out in this storm ain't like burrowing in coyote holes and chasing skunks," he pointed out. "I'm liable to freeze to death."

"You won't," Anna promised. "I've a plan."

His looked even more doubtful.

"At least listen." She scooted closer. "We'll tie together Top's rope and both of the jump ropes. Then we'll tie one end around your waist. Ida and me will stand on the stoop. We'll hold one end while you make your way to the lean-to. When you're ready, give the rope a yank and we'll pull you back. Karl will take the wood from you and stack it inside. If you get lost, we can reel you in. It'll be like fishing with a line and pole."

John Jacob snorted. "Only I don't cotton to being the bait—or the fish."

"We've gotta try, John Jacob." She cast her eyes around the room. "The littler ones won't survive the cold if we run out of wood."

He shrugged. "At home we all pile in one bed with a heap of quilts."

"Ain't no quilts here, John Jacob!" Anna fumed at his stubbornness.

Eloise shot her another impatient look. Anna smiled apologetically. Then she had another grand idea. Leaning her head over, she whispered into John Jacob's ear, "Miss Simmons will think you're a hero." She sat back, waiting for that to sink in.

"All right," he declared, jumping to his feet. "Tie me up!"

Anna leaped from the bench. "Miss Simmons," she shouted. "John Jacob's going out to get wood." When the teacher protested, Anna explained their need for wood and her plan to get it.

Miss Simmons rubbed her forehead. "Oh, I don't know about this. What if something happens to you, John Jacob?"

He thrust out his chest. "Don't you fret, Miss Simmons. I'm used to man's work."

"What about the cold?"

"I'll pile on the coats and gloves. Won't nothing happen to me."

"It should work, Miss Simmons," Ida said. "And Anna's right. We need the wood."

Again Miss Simmons hesitated. She patted the strands of hair escaping from her bun. She fiddled with a button.

"Well?" Anna prompted.

"Oh, all right," she reluctantly agreed. "I allow we have no choice."

Anna, Karl, Ida, and John Jacob put their boots back on and gathered any extra sweaters and coats. The other children quit listening to Eloise. They stole closer to watch the four bundle up.

Eloise stamped her foot to get their attention. "Listen! I'm reading the part where Lewis and Clark pour barrels of water down a prairie dog hole!" she hollered, but the others ignored her. Hattie offered Anna her fur-lined mittens. William gave John Jacob his long wool scarf and jacket.

The boys knotted the ropes together. Then Ida tied one end around John Jacob's waist. She tugged on it. "Good and tight."

"Ida and me promise we won't let go, John Jacob," Anna said solemnly. His wool cap was pulled way down over his eyebrows. William's scarf covered his mouth, but he nodded a reply.

Miss Simmons opened the door and everybody leaned forward to peer outside. The snow was swirling so thick and fast that Anna couldn't see beyond the stoop.

"It is a whiteout," Ida gasped.

"As thick as Ma's potato soup," John Jacob mumbled from behind the scarf.

"As white as my ma's clean sheets," Anna added, awestruck.

Miss Simmons inhaled sharply. "You children can *not* go out in that!"

"We must." Anna looked at John Jacob. "When you've an armful of wood and want to come back, tug on the rope twice."

"John Jacob, you must be sensible. If you get too cold, come in," Miss Simmons said as she hovered over him. First, she tucked his sleeves into his mittens. Then she pulled his cap farther over his ears. "Anna will count to keep track of how long it takes you to get to the lean-to and pick up the wood," she went on. "That way, she'll know if you're lost or in trouble."

He bobbed his bundled head. Then he stepped

outside. Holding onto the rope, Anna followed. Ida was right behind her. Karl waited in the doorway.

Without a backward glance, John Jacob stepped off the stoop into foot-deep snow. In a blink, he disappeared in the thickly falling flakes. Anna began to count.

Knees bent, she braced herself against the biting wind. She could feel John Jacob's weight on the end of the rope. She could feel Ida right behind her, one hand clutching her coattail. Slowly, Anna let the rope slide through her mitten-covered fingers.

It went limp as Anna reached the count of fifty. She hoped John Jacob had found the lean-to. Next trip would be easier because there would be tracks.

She kept counting.

A gust buffeted her and almost knocked her off her feet. The snow stung as if someone was pelting her with river sand. It blew up her nose and down her neck. She fought off the urge to brush it away. She didn't dare let go of the rope.

Finally, at the count of one hundred and forty, she felt two tugs. He was ready to come back!

"Reel him in!" she hollered over her shoulder to Ida. Hand over hand, Anna took up the slack. Her heart was pounding. She spotted a dim shape emerging from the fog of snow. The shape became John Jacob. His arms were stacked with wood. He'd made it!

Karl came onto the stoop and took the wood from John Jacob, who headed back out. Anna began counting again, starting from zero. Her fingers were stiff. Her face had no feeling. The snow whirled and danced until her head grew dizzy. No wonder folks got lost in weather like this!

At the count of one hundred and sixty, the rope jerked twice. Anna and Ida pulled John Jacob in. When he reappeared, his cheeks were bright red. His cap and shoulders were covered with snow. "You all right?" Anna hollered.

"One more trip," he mumbled from behind his scarf. Then with a nod, he turned and vanished.

Anna felt the line loosen. Her nose ran and a sneeze racked her. For a second she lost count. Where had she stopped? *One hundred,* she guessed, and began counting again from there. Oh, she wished Miss Simmons had put Ida in charge of counting!

"One hundred and sixty-seven, one hundred and sixty-eight," Anna murmured between chapped lips. The line was still slack. Why hadn't John Jacob tugged? Had she counted all wrong?

Goose bumps of cold, of *worry,* prickled her arms.

Slowly, she began to reel in the rope. Chills raced up her spine as she realized she couldn't feel any weight on the other end. Anna held her breath, fearing the worst. When the tip of the rope slithered across the snow into sight, she let out a cry. There was nothing attached to it.

John Jacob was gone!

CHAPTER NINE

Ida's fingers gripped Anna's shoulder. "Where is he?" she screamed in Anna's ear.

Anna shook her head, too numb to reply. She pulled off her frozen mittens. Awkwardly she tied the rope around her own waist. Then she faced Ida.

"Hold on to the rope," she yelled over the wind as she slid her hands back into the mittens. "I'm going after him."

Ida nodded. Her eyes, gleaming from below her cap, had a wild, frightened look.

Anna plunged off the stoop. The snow was deeper than she thought, and she plummeted into a drift. Catching herself, she scrambled to her feet. She floundered onward, following John Jacob's dwindling trail.

"John Jacob!" she hollered.

She stopped and called again. Turning in a circle, she yelled his name until her throat felt raw. The wind buffeted her from all sides, and soon she lost any sense of direction. Which way was the school? Which way was the lean-to? Panic started to creep into her chest and down her arms. She held tightly to the rope, knowing it was her way back. For a moment Anna thought about giving Ida the signal, but she put the thought out of her mind. She couldn't leave her best friend out here.

"John Jacob!" Anna shouted, but the only reply was the howling wind.

Tears sprang into her eyes. Her best friend was lost and it was all her fault.

Blindly she struck out again along the disappearing path. Suddenly the toe of her boot hit something solid. The lean-to! It was so covered with snow, she could barely see it. She patted along the boards until she found her way to the front. A drift half-filled the opening. She scooped out the top and bent over. John Jacob was huddled beside the sack of cow chips. When he saw Anna, his eyes widened over his ice-crusted scarf.

She waved at him. He crawled toward her. Grabbing his arm, she pulled him from the lean-to. Then she reached back in and hauled out the sack of cow chips.

"Hold on!" she screamed into the wind. He looped

the fingers of his wool gloves over the rope. She tugged twice on the line, hoping the others hadn't given up.

The rope grew taut. One step at a time, the two forged through the snow, following their lifeline. Anna trudged behind John Jacob, dragging the heavy sack. They finally reached the stoop, and both of them collapsed, exhausted.

Ida and Miss Simmons helped them to their feet. Karl took the sack. When they entered the school, everybody cheered. Top clomped over and puffed at Anna's frosted head.

She cracked a smile, her lips tight.

"Thank heavens!" Miss Simmons cried over and over as she and the other kids unwrapped John Jacob's layers and then helped Anna, Ida, and Karl from their snowy clothes.

Miss Simmons laid the wet coats and hats on the benches to dry. The four shivering adventurers huddled around the stove. Hattie and Ruth brought them a mug of hot tea to share, hoping to ease their chills.

John Jacob took a sip and handed the mug to Anna. He held up his fingers. The tips were red.

"F-f-f-frostnip," Anna said between chattering teeth. She was trembling so hard that she could barely hold the mug. She quickly passed it to Ida.

John Jacob scowled. "Not even frost*bite?*"

"Naw," Karl said. "We'd have needed to leave you out longer for that."

"Shucks no!" John Jacob slanted a shy grin Anna's way. "Thanks for coming after me. When I realized that the knot had come untied and the rope had disappeared, I thought I was done for."

Anna's cheeks reddened and she hunkered low on the bench. "Well, we needed those cow chips."

"One thing's for sure," Karl said. "I ain't going out in that blizzard ever again!"

"Amen," Ida said.

"We shouldn't have to." John Jacob hooked his thumb toward the stove. "There's fuel enough to get us through the night. Don't you think, Anna?"

He was asking her! Anna hid her pleased grin in her sleeve. She nodded.

Ruth and Hattie came over. "We've fixed a picnic," they said quietly.

Anna glanced over her shoulder. Miss Simmons's cloak was spread on the floor in front of the blackboard. The food they'd collected was arranged on the lids of the lunch pails.

Anna's mouth began to water. Karl jumped up. "Yee haw! Let's dig in. I'm famished."

All the children sat around the cloak. Miss Simmons placed her desk chair between William and George. The girls had cut everything in tiny pieces so no one would miss out. That meant each lid held a scant amount.

Anna stared at the meager morsels in front of her. *This will be our last until we're rescued,* she thought, *whenever that might be.*

"The girls set a fine table, wouldn't you say?" Miss Simmons asked cheerfully.

George's mouth drew down into a pout. William's brows bunched in a frown.

"This is *all?*" Carolina whined. Her lower lip was quivering.

"Why it's a fine meal!" Anna said quickly. "And they used their best china, too. Just for us!"

Hattie, Eloise, and Ruth beamed.

"Let's bow our heads and give thanks that we have a roof over our head and wood for the stove," Miss Simmons said.

"And pray that our families are home safe," Ida added quietly.

"And to say thank you Lord for this bountiful feast!" Sally Lil exclaimed. "Why this looks better'n my family's Sunday supper!"

Anna giggled even though she knew Sally Lil wasn't joshing.

Miss Simmons finished the prayer and Karl said, "Amen and dig *in!*"

Instantly hands darted toward the lids, and for a few minutes all was silent. Anna slowly ate each morsel of egg, sandwich, potato, and biscuit. Then she sucked on the slivers of jerked meat and pickle, making them last. She saved the dab of taffy for dessert. She put the plum in her pocket for Top.

"My, that was tasty." John Jacob smacked his lips noisily.

"Um, um." George rubbed his stomach. "I can't wait until supper."

"That *was* supper," William said.

"Was not."

"Was too. So don't be such an ungrateful hog," said William.

George pounced on him and they rolled across the cloak, rattling the tin lids.

Ida grabbed William and Miss Simmons grabbed George. "Time for a Learning Bee," Miss Simmons announced as she set George on his feet.

Anna groaned. Adventures and picnics were over. And here she'd almost grown to like school!

"Yuck, what smells?" Carolina complained.

"It's Top." Hattie pointed at the pony. A pile of manure steamed on the floor behind him. "Anna, clean up after your pony."

"Right now, Anna, before I grow ill!" Eloise held her nose. "Miss Simmons, does he *have* to be in here? He's an animal."

Anna jumped up. "And you, Eloise Baxter, are a whiney pants! That don't mean we'll put *you* out! Besides, unless you're aiming to make your way to the privy in this blizzard, you're going to have to drop your fancy drawers on the stoop!"

"On the stoop!" John Jacob chortled. The boys doubled over with laughter, slapping their legs and hooting.

Eloise's jaw dropped. "I will *never.*"

"Anna, Eloise, mind your manners," Miss Simmons scolded. "That is not polite conversation for ladies!"

Anna stomped across the floor. Top stood along the side wall, plucking old grass and weeds from the sod blocks.

Propping her fists on her hips, Anna stared at the manure. At home, she had shovel and pitchfork. Here she'd have to make do. She glanced around the room, her gaze landing on her slate. She hopped over a bench and picked it up. A smudged $14-7=$_____ was still written on it.

"Finally, I can put that problem to good use," Anna

muttered as she scooped up the manure with the slate. When she threw it out the door, the cold air nearly took her breath away. She was sure that the temperature had dropped even more. And although it was still early afternoon, the sky was as gray as granite.

Evening's coming on early, Anna thought. She wiped the slate in the snow. When she went back in to the schoolhouse, she had to push hard with both hands to close the door. Finally she got it latched and stepped back. The wind rattled and shook the door like an intruder demanding to be let in.

Anna hurried back to the warmth of the stove.

The children were standing in two lines in front of the blackboard. Miss Simmons had arranged them from tall to short. "Anna, you'll be on Eloise's team. Stand in between Eloise and Sally Lil."

"Why does she have to be on my team?" Eloise complained. "She gets all the answers wrong."

Anna ducked her head as she found her place in line.

"She does not get them all wrong." Sally Lil stomped on Eloise's boot toe.

"Ouch!" Eloise whined. "Miss Simmons, she—"

The teacher rapped the pointer on the desk. "Let's begin, shall we?"

"Thanks for sticking up for me, Sally Lil," Anna whispered. "But Eloise is right. I do get them all wrong."

"Not *all*," Sally Lil insisted.

"Is the first team ready?" Miss Simmons asked Ida. Beside her stood Karl, then John Jacob, Hattie, Carolina, and William.

Anna raised her hand. "Miss Simmons, the teams ain't even. I'll stand out."

"Oh do!" Eloise agreed.

"You're right, Anna. The teams aren't even." Miss Simmons handed Ida the sheet of questions. "Ida, you take my place and call out the questions while I stoke the stove. Karl, you will take Ida's place as captain of team one."

"M-m-me?" Karl sputtered, but John Jacob shoved him to the front of the line.

"Ready?" Ida held the sheet primly. She cleared her throat. "First question: on what date did Nebraska become the thirty-seventh state?"

Anna's stomach rolled.

"March 1, 1867," Karl declared proudly.

"That's correct, Karl. Eloise, if a wagon train travels ten miles in one day, how far will it travel in four days?" Ida continued.

Arithmetic! Anna's head began to pound. She heard the creak of the stove door.

"Miss Simmons, do you need help?" Anna called.

"No thank you. I'm all done." Slipping a shawl over

her shoulders, the teacher sat down. She slumped over her desk and held her head between her hands.

It was almost Anna's turn and her head pounded, too. She knew just how Miss Simmons felt.

As the others answered questions, Anna fidgeted. She chewed her nails. By the time it was her turn, she'd bitten them to the quick. *Please, Ida. Give me an easy one.*

"Anna, who is Grover Cleveland?"

"That is so easy," Eloise scoffed.

Beside her, Sally Lil whispered, "Everybody knows that one, Anna."

Everyone but me! thought Anna. Her head swam dizzily, and she blurted out the first answer that came into her mind. "The president of Nebraska!"

Eloise groaned.

"That question will go to John Jacob."

"Grover Cleveland is the president of the United States," John Jacob answered without hesitation.

"Anna, sit down, please."

As Anna walked around the end of the bench, Eloise kicked her in the shins. "Thanks for making us lose," she hissed.

Anna curled her fingers into a fist. She was taking aim at Eloise's nose when the light in the room dimmed. She turned toward Miss Simmons's desk. The teacher was sitting upright, staring at the kerosene lamp. The yellow flame was flickering.

"I've run out of kerosene," Miss Simmons said, sounding frightened.

Anna's gaze swung to the window. The panes were completely frosted. Rushing over, she rubbed hard with her sleeve. But when she peered outside, all was black. It looked as if night had already fallen.

She stepped away from the window. Shadows played along the walls as the flame in the lamp flickered. Then it went out, plunging the room into darkness.

CHAPTER TEN

Carolina began to whimper. "I'm scared, Miss Simmons."

"Everyone hold on to each other," Miss Simmons called out.

Anna's eyes quickly adjusted to the dark. She was used to collecting eggs before the sun came up.

"I'll open the stove door, Miss Simmons," she said. Now that the lamp was out, she realized a faint light was coming through the window. Using it to find her way, she inched past the benches to the stove. It was a sight easier than picking her way through roosting chickens.

She squatted and pulled open the door. A golden glow spilled across her lap and onto the floor.

Sighs swept through the room.

Anna threw in some cow chips, which quickly caught fire in the hot coals. Sally Lil crouched next to her. Her lips were blue.

"You warm enough?" Anna asked.

The little girl shook her head.

"Then why didn't you say something?"

"Pa always says, 'Complaining won't warm you, my Sally Gal!'"

"I'm cold, too, Anna," William said. He and George were standing behind her, hands stretched toward the flame. George nodded in agreement.

"Then let's bundle up!" Anna rose and went to the cloak corner. "We'll pretend we live in a cave," she said as she grabbed jackets and caps from the pegs and from the benches. "But a hungry bear ran in after us and stomped out our fire. So we have to wear everything we own."

"Is there anything to eat in the cave?" William asked hopefully.

"There's plenty of pretend food," Anna replied. "We hunted down a buffalo just yesterday. So we have fresh meat." She handed Sally Lil, William, and George their outer clothes.

"But there ain't no buffalo around here anymore," John Jacob said.

"Then we'll pretend our cave is farther West. Like Buffalo Bill."

Carolina, Eloise, Hattie, and Ruth carried a bench closer to the stove and sat down.

"*We're* not going to live in a cave," Eloise said, and her friends nodded in agreement. "We're pretending we live in a great stone castle. Like those kings and queens in Great Britain."

William snorted. "I'd druther live in a cave."

Ida, Karl, and John Jacob joined them around the mouth of the stove. Everyone argued about which pretend place was the best. Soon the group was toasty warm.

Anna peered over her shoulder. Miss Simmons was still hunched over her desk in the dark. Anna thought about checking to see if the teacher was all right. But it was too cozy by the stove.

"How many people want to live in a damp old cave?" Eloise asked. "Raise your hands."

Anna's hand shot up first. Then Karl, John Jacob, William, and George raised their hands. Sally Lil slowly lifted hers, too. Anna grinned at Eloise. For once, she'd gotten more of the kids on her side!

Eloise jumped up. "Oh, who cares about a pretend place anyway? I have something better. A *surprise*."

1068885654

"What, Eloise?" Ruth and Hattie chorused. "Tell us!"

Eloise smiled coyly. "I brought it from home. I was saving it for later."

"It is later!" George declared.

"Now. We want it *now!*" William demanded.

"Let me make sure it's all right with Miss Simmons." Eloise went over to the teacher and whispered something in her ear. Miss Simmons nodded and opened the top drawer of her desk. She drew out a flat box and handed it to Eloise.

When Eloise came back to the stove, everyone flocked around her. "Let us see," they all said. "What is it?"

Could it be a picture? Anna wondered. *A book?* She craned her neck to get a better look.

"Stop crowding round and I'll show you." Eloise sat on the bench. Everyone stared at the box balancing on her knees. Eloise smoothed her skirt. She patted her lacy collar. She retied her hair ribbon.

"Eloise, get on with it!" Ida finally snapped.

"You don't have to be so pushy," Eloise retorted. Then she smiled and said, "It's a board game."

"A game?" Karl repeated. "Probably a stupid girl game."

"Called the Mansion of Happiness," Eloise said, ignoring him.

Twitters of excitement arose from the girls.

Hattie clapped her hands. "Oh, I've heard it's such fun!"

"Open it, Eloise. Please do!" Carolina begged.

With great care, Eloise removed the lid. Slowly she pulled out a flat board and unfolded it. Anna leaned closer. The light from the stove spilled across a spiral of colorful pictures and shapes painted on the board. In the center was a picture of a fashionably dressed family. Anna blinked in amazement. So *this* was a board game. She'd never seen anything like it before!

Eloise began explaining the game rules. "You spin this wooden top to see how many spaces you can move. You try to be the first player to reach the center of the board. That's Eternal Happiness. That means happiness *forever.*"

"*Forever,*" Carolina repeated breathlessly.

"Eternal happiness?" jeered Karl. "I'd much rather play marbles."

"Be quiet," said Carolina. "Let Eloise finish."

"The only trouble is that not *everyone* can play at one time." Eloise's gaze went pointedly to Anna.

With a jolt, Anna sat back on her heels. "Oh, that's

all right. I'll stand out this game," she offered.

She stood up and strode over to Top, blinking back her tears. "Who cares about Eloise's old game," she muttered angrily, burying her face in the pony's mane. "Surely not *me*. I'd rather be tending my sheep." She thought about her small flock. Were they trapped in the drifting snow, shivering in the wind? "Oh, Top," she snuffled. "I hope Mama thought to get them in."

A tug on her sleeve made Anna turn around. It was Sally Lil. She clutched Anna's jacket around her bony shoulders. No one, not even Anna, would lend her a cap. Lice were too pesky to get rid of.

Anna wiped her eyes, glad it was dark. She didn't want Sally Lil to see her tears.

"Will you let me sit on Top?" the little girl asked. "I ain't never ridden a pony."

"Why sure. But don't you want to play the game?" Anna looked toward the others. They sat in the circle of warmth, huddled around the board.

Sally Lil shrugged. "Naw. I don't want happiness forever. Just a ride on your pony."

"We can't go far."

Sally Lil's eyes gleamed in the stove light. "Far enough for me!"

Anna boosted her on Top. Since there was no bridle

or rope, she twined her fingers in the pony's fuzzy mane. Clucking, she led him along the back wall. A gust of wind rattled the door when they passed by.

Anna shuddered. "I'm glad I ain't out there. It's cold enough in here."

Sally Lil was grinning too hard to reply.

George waddled over wearing his thick coat. "Hey," he said, "I want a ride too!" His wool cap almost covered his eyes, and he tilted back his head to stare up at Sally Lil.

"No, George. You go on back to playing the game," Sally Lil said stubbornly.

"Naw. Eloise is too bossy for me."

"You can have a ride when Sally is done. There're turns for all," Anna said. "Walking will keep us warm."

When they reached the coat corner, Anna turned the pony slowly. Still, he knocked over several lunch pails. She halted him at the water bucket. Making a fist, she broke through the crust of ice.

"Don't tell," she whispered to Sally Lil when Top dipped his head for a drink.

They started off again. George clomped beside Anna in his big boots. Sally Lil's skinny legs wrapped tightly around the pony's fat sides. "Oh, this is joyous!" she exclaimed.

They started past the door, which strained at its latch. *Cre-e-eak.* The rusty hinges screeched. *Like haunts trying to get in,* Anna thought with a shudder.

Clucking to Top, Anna hurried him past the door. She tripped over a log and stumbled into George.

Crash! A thunderous bang echoed through the room.

Anna spun around in time to see the door fly inward. For an instant it flapped wildly. Then it tore from its hinges and fell on the floor with a whump. Before Anna could react, a swirl of wind caught the door, lifted it, and carried it through the doorway where it disappeared into the storm.

Anna stared, shocked by the gaping hole. The wind had blown the door away like it was a sheet of paper!

"Gee whilliky crickets!" George gasped.

"What happened, what happened?" Miss Simmons hurried from the front of the room. Her cheeks were flushed as if she had a fever. She clasped her shawl tightly around her throat.

"The door just up and flew away," Anna said. "I've never seen anything like it."

"Oh my." Miss Simmons pressed one hand to her cheek. "Oh *my.*"

By then the others had left the game to see what was going on. Everybody stared at the snow pouring through the open doorway like flour tossed from a bucket.

"What'll we do?" Karl asked.

"Ain't nothing we can do," John Jacob replied. "Door's *gone.*"

"There must be something we can use to block the doorway," Ida said. "How about the blackboard?"

"Absolutely not. That blackboard cost the town a pretty penny," Eloise said, sounding like her father.

"Shut up, Eloise," Ida said crossly. "It's either the blackboard or freezing to death."

Eloise set her hands on her hips. "Who wants to keep playing?" she asked as she marched back to the game board. Hattie, Ruth, Carolina, and William followed her.

"Ida, your suggestion was excellent, but the blackboard took three grown men to hang," Miss Simmons said quietly. "And without hammer and nails to secure it, I'm afraid the wind will blow it away, too."

Despair shone in Ida's eyes. "We can't sit here and freeze to death!"

Miss Simmons slid one arm around Ida's shoulder. In silence, the group watched the snowflakes rushing toward them.

"We best move to the front of the room," Anna said.

"Let the snow fill up the doorway. Maybe it'll keep the wind out and the heat in. Like an igloo."

"Why, Anna, I'm glad you remembered that lesson." Miss Simmons said.

"That's how my grandpa survived one winter in the war," Karl said. "He dug a home in the snow."

"Let's get everything to the front then," John Jacob said, reaching for the handle of the water bucket.

"Come on, Sally Lil. Top will move you." Anna led the pony alongside the outer wall. John Jacob followed behind with the bucket and dipper. The other boys carried lunch pails filled with snow to melt for drinking water. Ida and Miss Simmons gathered every stray mitten, rag, cap, and boot.

"Whoa, Top." Anna halted the pony in a far corner. Top didn't need to be close to the stove. As long as he was out of the wind, his fluffy coat would keep him warm.

"Slide off, Sally Lil," Anna said.

"Nope." She stretched out on his neck. "I'm staying here forever. He's my fur blanket."

Anna grinned. "I reckon he can be your bed for the night."

She hurried back to the coat corner and retrieved Top's bridle and the long rope they'd used for John

Jacob. She put them on the floor beside the pony so they wouldn't get buried in the snow. Then she went to help John Jacob move the other benches. She heard arguing coming from the Mansion of Happiness.

"You took two turns, Carolina," Eloise was saying.

"Did not."

"Did too."

"Did too," William chimed in.

Eloise jumped up. "I'm quitting and when Papa comes, I'm taking my game home with me."

Carolina began to cry. "I want to go home, too."

"Even if the snow stops, it'll be too dark to go home," John Jacob told her. "With no lantern, we'd get lost for sure."

Carolina's wail grew louder.

Miss Simmons rubbed her temples. "Children, *please.*"

"Ida, why don't we get everyone to play Button Button?" Anna suggested. The older girl was sitting on the bench on the other side of the stove. Her lap was filled with caps and mittens, and she was staring into the fire.

"Ida?" Anna repeated.

When Ida didn't reply, Anna sat beside her. "Are you all right?"

Ida plucked listlessly at the caps and scarves. Her lips and cheeks were pale.

"I reckon you're cold." Picking up one of the scarves, Anna wrapped it around Ida's shoulders. "Better?"

She barely nodded.

"Ida, you must stay strong," Anna said, growing worried. "We need to be brave for the littler ones. Or soon they'll all be whining to go home."

"I'm trying," Ida whispered, tears welling in her eyes. "But sometimes this godforsaken place beats me down, Anna."

Anna's mouth fell open. She was used to Mama saying such things, not Ida.

"And when I'm beaten down I can't muster even a speck of brave." Arms hugging her sides, Ida rocked on the bench. "Then I grow afraid. Afraid of the dark, the wind, the snow, the cold. I *try* to be brave." The tears spilled from her eyes and rolled down her cheeks. "But I'm *not*. Oh, Anna, I want to go home, too!"

CHAPTER ELEVEN

For a moment, Anna was too surprised to reply. Ida always acted so strong and true. She cared for her brothers and sisters when Mrs. Friesen was bedridden with a newborn baby. She milked the cows and chopped wood when Mr. Friesen worked in town for extra money. Never had Anna seen John Jacob's older sister so glum. Not even when she'd lost the district spelling bee!

"Ida, it's all right if you're not *always* brave," she said, patting her shoulder clumsily. "Why, you care for your family. You read a book a day. You cipher long division. And you know all the presidents."

"Scant help in the middle of a snowstorm," Ida choked out as she dabbed her eyes with a mitten.

Anna frowned, not sure how to make Ida feel better. She glanced around. A drift now partially blocked the doorway, but snow still blew in from the top, dusting the floor and walls. In the front of the room, Miss Simmons sat at her desk, comforting Carolina.

"I bet the storm will be over soon." Anna said, turning back to Ida. "Then we can all go home. John Jacob said it'll be too dark, but we can make torches with pieces of firewood. Until then, you must try to stop crying. If the littler ones hear you, they'll be crying, too."

Ida pressed the mitten to her mouth.

"Maybe there's more hot tea." Anna went over to the kettle. The rest of the children were slumped on a bench angled beside the stove. Hattie and Ruth leaned against each other, sniffing sadly. The boys sat stooped over, their elbows on their knees. Eloise twirled a stray lock of hair, the closed game box on her lap.

"What a lot of gloomy faces!" Anna exclaimed. "I thought everyone would be excited about playing Button Button."

"I'm too cold to play," Hattie said.

"I'm too hungry."

"I'm too tired."

"What's this I hear? No one wants to play?" Ida came up beside Anna, a button nestled in the palm of her mitten. There was no trace of her tears. "And here I found a button."

Anna gave Ida's arm a quick squeeze.

"Oh, who wants to play with a dirty button," Eloise grumbled.

"Me." Sally Lil appeared out of the shadows. "I *love* Button Button."

Karl snorted. "You love every old thing."

"I'll play if I can be 'It' first," Eloise said, setting the game box on the floor.

"That's fine. Now everyone sit in a row on the bench. Carolina?" Ida called into the dark. "Why don't you come join us?"

Carolina ran over and squeezed in between Hattie and Ruth. Everyone took off their gloves and mittens and held their hands out, palms together. Eloise stood in front, the button between her two palms.

Slowly she walked in front of the bench, passing her hands between each player's outstretched hands. When it was her turn, Anna held her hands lightly together. Eloise passed her palms between Anna's, and Anna felt the button slip into her hands. She caught her breath. Eloise had given the button to her first!

When Eloise reached the end of the bench, she chanted, "Button, button, who's got the button?" Everyone took a turn guessing.

"John Jacob," Karl said.

John Jacob shook his head.

"Ida!" Hattie shouted.

"No, it's Ruth!" Anna held back a giggle.

Soon all the names had been called except Anna's.

Eloise grinned smugly. "Ha, ha, I fooled you all. Anna has the button. I knew no one would guess her. That means I get a second time to be 'It'."

Anna's joy faded. And here she thought Eloise had picked her special. She gave Eloise the button, but the game didn't seem fun anymore. Not even when John Jacob passed her the button on his turn.

Beside Anna, Sally Lil yawned loudly. Her head slumped to Anna's shoulder. Soon the whole line of children was yawning. Miss Simmons came over. The teacher had been so quiet that Anna was startled to see her.

"I see some sleepyheads," Miss Simmons said. "Who's ready for bed?" She gestured behind her. Under the blackboard, she'd spread newspapers and rags on the rug. "It's not a feather mattress," she apologized. "But the papers and rags should ward off the damp. If we pile together, we can keep warm."

Cheering and hooting, the children hopped off the bench. They scrambled for a place on the rug.

"Keep on your coats and hats," Miss Simmons went

on. "We can use my cloak for a cover. Boots and scarves will have to do for pillows."

Hattie, Ruth, Eloise, and Carolina snuggled together. Miss Simmons spread the cloak over them. Sally Lil tried to find a spot by them, but they pushed her away.

"Come lie down next to me," Miss Simmons said. She sat on the floor, her back against the desk, her skirts arranged in a ladylike way. Sally Lil lay her head in the teacher's lap, and Miss Simmons covered her with the end of her shawl.

After a few minutes of wrestling, even the boys piled raggedly against each other. Only Ida and Anna hung back.

"Anna? Ida? There's room." Miss Simmons waved at a sliver of space beside Sally Lil.

"I'm going to sleep with Top," Anna said.

"I'll stay up and watch the stove," Ida said. "We can't let it go out."

"Thank you, Ida," Miss Simmons said. "Wake me when you tire, and we'll switch places."

"Yes ma'am." Ida pulled the desk chair up to the stove. She opened her book. Miss Simmons rested her head against the side of the desk and closed her eyes.

Anna joined her pony in the corner. In the spring, she and Top often stayed out on the prairie with the sheep. When the nights were chilly, they'd curl up together for warmth and companionship.

"Come on, Top," she whispered. "Time to bed down." Using two fingers, she tapped behind his front knee. The pony folded his legs and sank to the floor. Anna wriggled between his bent legs. She laid her head on his bulgy stomach. The floor was hard and the chill seeped through her stockings.

"I know this ain't like sleeping in sweet prairie grass," she told Top as she drew her legs under her skirt. "But we'll have to make do."

She yawned. The pony's heat flowed through her and her eyelids grew heavy. In the dim glow of the stove, she could see the others on the floor. They were nestled together like puppies in a basket. Then she turned her gaze to Miss Simmons and Ida.

Outside, the blizzard beat angrily on the sod walls. Inside, Ida silently turned the pages of her book. Miss Simmons stroked Sally Lil's cheek.

Anna hoped that she would grow up to be as smart as Ida and as kind and pretty as Miss Simmons. *And,* she decided before falling asleep, *I hope to be as brave as they are, too.*

✳✳✳✳✳

A scream woke Anna. She jerked to a sitting position. Snow pelted her bare cheeks. Top scrambled to his feet, and she tipped over, falling clumsily under his belly.

Another shriek sent goose bumps skittering up Anna's arms. She crawled from underneath Top, grabbed hold of his mane, and pulled herself to her feet. It was so dark, she couldn't see anything but the snow swirling around her.

Panic muddled her head. *How did I get outside in the blizzard?*

She heard Sally Lil cry out. "Anna! Anna! Where are you?"

"Sally Lil?" *Is she outside, too?*

Anna let go of Top and forced her feet to move forward. Her toe stubbed against something hard. She felt around with her gloved fingers. It was the desk.

She reared back, utterly confused. She *wasn't* outside. But where then?

"Anna? Over here!"

She glanced in the direction of the voice. A faint light shone through the curtain of snow. She stumbled toward it. Top whickered and clomped behind her.

"Anna!"

When she got closer to the light, she saw John Jacob,

Karl, and Ida standing in front of the stove. Anna's jaw dropped when she realized where she was. She was still inside the school!

"What happened?" she yelled.

"The roof!" Ida pointed overhead. "Part of it caved in!"

"The roof?" Anna tilted back her head. The stovepipe rose into nothingness. The windswept snowflakes stung her eyes. "Where are the others?" she asked.

John Jacob jabbed his thumb toward the back of the school. "On the rug. We need to gather everyone around the stove. The walls might collapse next."

Anna shuddered at the thought. Sticking close together, the four made their way to the jumble of children on the floor. Most were awake and crying out. Ida bent to help Hattie, Eloise, and Ruth put on their boots. Karl knelt by William and George. John Jacob found the broom and began sweeping snow off the top of the stove.

Miss Simmons was still sitting on the floor by the desk. Sally Lil and Carolina were clinging to her waist, weeping. Anna crouched over them. "With the roof falling in, the school isn't safe anymore," she yelled in the teacher's ear. "We have to find other shelter."

"But where?" Miss Simmons seemed on the verge of tears. "The blizzard is still raging."

Anna fought back her own panic. "I don't know. But we can't stay here."

Miss Simmons nodded and got up. "Come, girls," she said, "let's get your boots."

Anna stood. She turned in a circle, hopelessness spinning around her like the wind. Earlier, the school had been the safest place. But with no door or roof, it was safe no longer. If they stayed there they would freeze.

But where would they go? And how would they get there?

Even with the light from the stove, Anna could barely see in front of her. How would they find their way through the storm?

Top Hat nudged Anna's shoulder with his nose. Anna brushed the snow off the pony's head. "I know, Top," she whispered. "I want to go home, too." She stared into his brown eyes.

Top Hat!

Top would lead them! Didn't he always find the sheep in the dark of early morning? Didn't he sense the trail home after a long night?

The Friesens' farm was not even a mile from the

schoolhouse. Top had taken Anna there more times than she could count. Anna was sure he could lead them now.

"Miss Simmons!" Anna stepped across William's legs and hurried to the teacher, who was bent over lacing Sally Lil's boots.

"We can get to the Friesens'," Anna said. "It's less than a mile. Top knows the way. He'll lead us there."

"Top? Yes, Top!" Sally Lil cried.

Ida frowned. She was clutching Hattie and Ruth's hands. "Should we leave the stove?" she asked. "It's our only light. Our only way to keep warm."

"We *can't* leave," Eloise wailed. "My pa won't know where to find me."

John Jacob spoke up. "Listen everyone. We have to leave. The snow's falling too hard for the stove to keep up. And the wind is blowing so hard, the stovepipe might collapse and maybe even the walls."

Carolina began to cry again.

"John Jacob's right. Everyone put on your scarves and mittens," Ida said. "Stuff rags and newspaper up your coats."

Anna made her way to the corner, Top right beside her. Stooping, she felt around for the rope and her pony's bridle. When she found them, she held the metal bit beneath her arm to warm it.

Miss Simmons came up and wrapped her shawl around Anna's shoulders.

"I'm fine," Anna said, although chills racked her.

"You lent Sally Lil your coat. Now I'll lend you mine," Miss Simmons said. She knotted the shawl at Anna's throat. "I've my cloak to wear."

"Thank you, ma'am." Anna busied herself with bridling Top. Despite her stiff, fumbling fingers, he took the bit. She slipped the headpiece over his ears.

When Top's bridle was in place, Anna handed the coil of rope to Miss Simmons. "Lash as many children together as you can," she told her. "That way, no one will get lost." Then Anna joined Karl, Ida, and John Jacob, who were using lunch pails and slates to scoop away the snow from the doorway.

Miss Simmons tied Eloise to Hattie, Hattie to Ruth, and Ruth to William. Then she tied William to George and George to Karl before the rope ran out. By that time, Anna and the others had cleared a narrow path through the snowdrift.

"The two little girls can ride Top," Anna said. She boosted Sally Lil onto the pony.

Carolina whimpered. "No time for tears," John Jacob declared, tossing her up behind Sally Lil.

Miss Simmons gave the end of the rope to Ida, who looped it around her arm.

"Hold on to Top's tail, Ida," Anna said. "And don't let go."

"I'll go last," Miss Simmons said, "to watch out for stragglers."

John Jacob shook his head. "No, ma'am. I'll bring up the rear. That's a gentleman's job."

"No, John Jacob," she protested. "I can't let you go last. It's a teacher's duty."

He nodded firmly. "No Ma'am. You keep hold of the littler ones."

"Everybody ready?" Anna asked. There was a chorus of muffled replies. "I'm going to take a look outside first."

Anna pulled her cap over her ears and stepped onto the stoop. The wind struck her like a hammer. It threw her against the doorjamb like she was nothing but a stick. Behind her, the two little girls on Top shrieked.

Anna sucked in a frosty breath. Stunned, she stared into the night. All she could see was a swirling mass of windblown snow. The walls of the school had protected them from the wind, Anna realized. Here, outside, it rushed across the plains like a furious beast.

Her heart sank. There was no way they'd make it to the Friesens' farm. The icy blasts would sweep them to the open prairie where they'd freeze to death. Or it would drive them toward the river where they could fall through the ice and drown.

Turning, she hollered back to Ida, "It's no use! We'd never make it!"

Ida nodded in agreement. She and Miss Simmons helped Sally Lil and Carolina off Top and herded everybody back to the stove.

"What do we do now?" Ida asked.

Suddenly a shrill, grinding noise made Anna look up. She felt someone shove her and she stumbled backward. The top of the stovepipe crashed where she'd been standing.

"Are you all right?" asked John Jacob. "I'm sorry I had to push you so hard."

"I-I think so," Anna gasped. Smoke, pushed low by the wind, whipped around her head.

"The stovepipe's split in two. We *have* to leave," John Jacob shouted in Anna's ear. "Before the smoke gets too thick!"

"But out there is hopeless." Anna heard the whine in her voice. *Oh no,* she thought, *I sound just like Eloise!*

"Then we must think of something, Anna." John Jacob leaned closer. A smile creased his cold-reddened cheeks. "Ain't you the one who's always up for an adventure?"

She heard the challenge and gave him a shaky grin. "I guess we'll just have to figure out a way to outfox the storm. Think hard, John Jacob. How can we keep it from blowing us all to kingdom come?"

"We have to make sure we start out in the right direction. And stay on course…at least until we get to our shed," John Jacob said.

A thought struck Anna. *The barbed wire fence!*

She gripped his arm. "The fence! It runs along the lane to your shed. We can use it to guide our way to your farm."

"Yes. *Yes!*" John Jacob punched his fist in his gloved palm.

Excitement filled Anna, warming her toes and fingers. "Tell the others. Top and I are going out to find the fence."

"*No.* Not alone."

Anna pulled the shawl tighter around her shoulders and rushed toward the door before he could stop her. Snatching up the dangling rein, she led Top onto the stoop. She brushed the snow off his forelock and whispered in his bent ear, "I'm counting on you, Top."

Grabbing mane, Anna vaulted onto her pony's back. Then she dug her heels in his sides and together they plunged into the blinding snow.

CHAPTER TWELVE

Knees reaching high, Top plowed through the drifts. The snow brushed his belly and lapped the toes of Anna's boots. She clung to his mane, unable to see past the pony's ears. She had to guess the direction of the fence.

Suddenly Top halted, almost tossing Anna over his head. She righted herself and thrust out her hand. Her glove snagged on something sharp. It was the barbed wire fence!

Anna whooped. She steered Top back toward the school. The pony lunged down the trail they'd made, up onto the stoop, and through the doorway.

"We found it. We found it!" Anna shouted as she slid off Top. Everybody crowded around. "We found the fence. It can lead us to the Friesens'!"

She lifted Sally Lil onto Top, and John Jacob put Carolina on behind. Carolina wrapped her arms around Sally Lil's skinny waist. Her lower lip trembled. She coughed when the thick smoke blew in her face.

"I'll make sure Carolina doesn't fall off," Sally Lil said, trying to sound brave.

Loud thuds made Anna spin sideways. The front wall of the schoolhouse, buffeted by the wind, was sagging inward. Sod blocks were dropping to the floor like sacks of wet flour.

"Go! Go!" John Jacob yelled.

Clucking to Top, Anna guided him off the stoop. The thigh-deep snow dragged at her skirts, and she floundered along beside the pony. She glanced over her shoulder. Sally Lil and Carolina were one lump on Top's back. She couldn't see past the pony's rump. She prayed that the others were right behind.

When Anna reached the end of the beaten-down path, she searched for the barbed wire. This time her coat sleeve caught in the barbs.

"Ida!" she screamed into the raging wind. "We're at the fence line. Do you have hold of Top's tail?"

"Yes!" came her faint reply.

"Are the others still behind you?"

"Yes!"

"Then we'll move on!" Anna turned to the left. With her right hand, she felt for the fence. She couldn't keep her hand on it; the barbs were too sharp. She'd just have to keep checking to make sure they didn't wander too far from the fence and get lost.

Anna urged the pony forward. Head tucked, she battled her way through the fresh snow. One hand gripped Top's rein; the other gripped his neck.

One, two, three, four, five, Anna counted her strides. On the fifth step, she reached for the fence. Her hand hit a wooden post, its top hidden by the drifted snow. She didn't dare wait past five. One wrong step could lead them astray.

One, two, three, four, five. Counting helped keep Anna's mind from growing as numb as her feet. Snow clung to her stockings and skirt and made them heavy. Her gloves and boots were frozen stiff. Her cheeks and ears had lost all feeling.

Beside her, Top strode steadily. His nostrils flared pink, and icicles hung from his muzzle hairs. When Anna stumbled and fell in a drift, he waited patiently until she pulled herself up.

One, two, three, four, five. Anna reached out for the fence again, but felt nothing. She swatted in all directions. *Where is it?* Then her elbow whacked the top strand, and tears of relief welled in her eyes. Quickly, she checked on Sally Lil and Carolina, who were as white as snowmen.

"Are you all right?" she shouted.

Sally Lil nodded.

Taking a deep breath, Anna set off again, breaking through an icy crust. Her knees and legs ached and each stride grew harder.

One, two, three… Her counting slowed. *Four…five…* Anna stopped to catch her breath. Snow slithered down her neck. She could no longer feel her feet.

How much farther? Straightening, she stared in front of her. She had no idea how far they'd walked or how far they had to go. All landmarks, all *distance,* had been erased by the whitewash of snow.

Pea soup. That's what Mama called fog. Oh, this was much worse!

"Ida!" Anna cried, flakes whirling into her mouth.

"We're okay!" Ida screamed back.

I'm not, Anna thought. Her chest heaved. She tried to take a step, but her boots felt nailed to the ground.

I'm so cold. So tired. She closed her eyes just for a minute and leaned against Top's neck. She listened to the soft *shush, shush* of the falling snow. It sounded like Mama humming a lullaby.

Anna's mind drifted; her body swayed. Suddenly, someone pushed her roughly. Anna toppled into the snow. It closed around her, choking her. She clawed free. Top stood over her like a snowy beast.

"What are you doing?" Anna yelled angrily. He pawed the snow at her feet. Then he lowered his head to push her again, and she hit him on the nose. Grabbing the cheek strap of the bridle, she pulled herself up.

"Stop it, Top. Stop it!" she screamed. Then she gasped, realizing what Top had done. *He'd saved her life.*

Anna had heard tales of folks falling asleep in the snow. *Falling asleep and never waking.*

She hugged him. "Oh, Top. *You* know we can't stop. You know we have to keep going no matter what."

Spring, summer, and fall, Anna and Top guarded the flock. In all their years together, they'd never lost one sheep. Top was making sure they wouldn't lose one now.

Anna stomped her feet, flapped her arms, and slapped her cheeks. *I might not be smart or brave,* she thought. *But I know what needs to be done.*

Anna clucked to Top. "One…two…three… four…five…" she counted aloud, ignoring the snow beating against her. They had to keep moving a little longer, then they could rest. She put her head down against the wind and forced her numb feet to take five more steps. Then five more.

"One...two...three—" Anna's shoulder bumped a wooden post. Immediately past the post, she ran into a hard, solid corner. It was the shed!

"Hurry, Top." She inched her way along the rough wooden wall. The three-sided shed was used for storing wood and cow chips. Where was the open side? Finally Anna realized that the opening was drifted shut. Holding on to Top, she plowed through the snow back to Ida. The older girl was hunched over like an old woman. Snow completely covered her clothes. All Anna could see was her eyes.

"I found the shed." She leaned into the wind toward Ida. "How far is it to the house?"

"About a hundred steps. Straight ahead and to the right."

"You'll have to lead the way, Ida. The fence stops. There's nothing to guide me."

Ida shook her head. "I c-c-can't, Anna." Her teeth chattered. "My skirts are f-frozen stiff. I c-c-can't move my legs! Top's been dragging me."

"Oh, Ida." Anna moaned. Behind Ida, she could

barely make out a dim shape. That had to be Karl. The rest were invisible.

"John Jacob!" Anna hollered. There was no answer. Panic filled her. What if the others had come untied?

"Anna," Ida whispered feebly. "We *must* k-k-keep moving. Or none of us will make it."

"Yes, all right." Anna nodded. "I'll find the way."

I'll find the way. Brave words. But this time, there would be no fence to guide her.

She'd have to rely on Top.

The pony stood quietly, his head bowed, the two girls slumped over on his back. Snow had crusted over his nostrils and eyes. "Oh, Top." Anna gently brushed off his face. She laid her cheek against his. "Don't you give up!"

The pony shook and icicles tinkled in the air. Anna tried to make a clucking noise, but her lips were too stiff. "C-come, Top. You've got to find the Friesens'." She tugged on the reins and side by side they trudged forward.

Anna prayed they were headed in the right direction.

She began counting to a hundred. A hundred steps and they should reach the Friesens' house.

As she walked, the wind pummeled her to and fro. She held tightly to Top's mane. The cold bit through her clothes. The snow clung like weights on her legs.

Top kept walking. Anna stumbled beside him.

One hundred. She stopped counting. She rubbed the snow from her face with a crusty glove. She stared right. Left. Straight ahead.

There was nothing.

She'd led them to *nothing.*

They were lost on the prairie in the middle of a blizzard. *And it was her fault.*

Anna sunk down in the snow. She raised her head to the sky and wailed like a lone coyote. "No-no-no."

"Ann-na!"

A cry came from far away. Anna held her breath. Was she hearing things?

"Ann-na!"

No, someone *was* calling her name!

Anna stood up clumsily. "Here! Over here!"

Top pricked his ears. Raising his head, he whinnied.

"Anna! Don't move!"

Papa? Could it be?

"We'll come to you, Anna!"

It is Papa!

Anna wanted to run screaming toward her father's voice. Only where was his voice coming from? She swung right, then left. With trembling fingers she pushed her stiff cap from her ears. Howling from all sides deafened her. Oh, the wind was playing tricks!

Then she saw it. A golden glow moving toward her. A lantern!

"Papa! Straight ahead!" Anna shouted.

Turning, she shook Sally Lil's and Carolina's legs. "Help's coming! It's coming!" There was no sound from the girls.

A sob caught in her throat. *Don't let it be too late!*

"Anna!" The light dazzled her. "Oh, my child!" Arms closed around her, and Anna fell weeping against her father's snowy chest.

"Papa, the roof blew off the school. We had to come."

"Mister Friesen's with me. He's pulling a sled."

Ida and John Jacobs's father came up, the sled gliding behind him. Anna wanted to stay forever in the safety of her father's arms. But she pulled away and said tearfully, "When we left, everyone was tied together behind Top. But I couldn't see them. I couldn't see them, Papa." She broke down, her sobs shaking her shoulders. "Oh, I hope they're all right."

Papa squeezed her shoulder. "Stay by Top," he instructed as he handed her his lantern. Anna swayed against the pony. Through blurry eyes, she watched as her father and Mister Friesen disappeared in the icy whirl.

For what seemed like forever, she waited, shivering with the cold, with *sorrow*. Oh, what if her friends had not made it!

Then Mister Friesen reappeared, pulling Ruth, Eloise, and Hattie on the sled. Papa was right behind. George was in his arms. William clung to his back.

Anna cried out, this time with joy.

"Bring Top and the lantern and walk right behind me," Papa shouted as he strode past. "The others will follow. It's not far."

Moments later, Anna spotted a rectangle of light shining like a star through the fog of snow. Mrs. Friesen stood, a dark silhouette, in the open doorway of the soddy. She began to cry when she spotted the children.

The snow had been packed down in front of the house. Anna halted Top under a protective roof. The pony's sides heaved. She hobbled around behind him, her feet like stumps and her toes crackling like twigs. Ida, Miss Simmons, and John Jacob appeared through the snow.

They'd made it!

Ida collapsed in her mother's arms. John Jacob fell to his knees. Miss Simmons blinked as if in a daze.

"We made it, Miss Simmons." Anna took the teacher's arm and led her to the doorway. Then she went back to help John Jacob, who was still kneeling on the hard-packed snow.

She grasped his elbow.

With frosty mittens, he tugged his scarf away from his mouth. "I can get up myself, thank you. I was trying to kiss the good earth, but my lips are too froze. I'll just have to thank the Lord instead."

A giggle bubbled in Anna's chest. "I was worried I'd lost you in a drift somewhere, John Jacob. Like we'd been playing Crack the Whip and you'd been flung off!"

"Why, I've never been flung off," he retorted as he struggled to his feet. Then his blue lips tipped up in a grin. "When the snow quits tomorrow, I bet we can find some frozen prairie chickens."

"And dig a snow fort."

"And go sledding." John Jacob grinned wider at Anna. She grinned back, wincing as the skin on her chapped lips cracked. "Well, I gotta get out of these boots," he said, "and inspect my toes. Might be this time I got frost*bite.*"

Still smiling, Anna watched him limp into the house.

Papa passed him in the doorway. "You gave us a scare, Miss Anna," he said.

"I gave myself a scare," she replied. "Rattlers, coyotes, grasshoppers, drought. Why, they're nothing compared to this blizzard. Are Mama and Little Seth all right?"

"Snug as those bedbugs your mama hates."

"And what about the sheep?"

"Mama saw the clouds and drove them home. Now quit fretting and come inside." He pulled off her wool cap. It had frozen into the shape of a bowl. "Missus Friesen can pour you some soup in this," he joked, then he pulled her tight against his heavy coat. "Mister Friesen and I tried to get through to the school earlier, but the wind beat us back. When there was a slight letup, we decided to try again. We were so afraid…" His words lodged in his throat.

"I know, Papa," Anna whispered into his buttons. "I know."

"Come on, let's get you in where it's warm." Arm around her shoulder, Papa led her toward the open door.

"Wait." Anna looked around. "Where's Top? I ain't leaving him out in this storm."

He chuckled. "Come on inside." Gently he steered her into the house.

The Friesens' two-room soddy was bursting with

children and wet clothes. Top stood in the middle of it all, munching a forkful of hay.

Anna's jaw dropped. John Jacob's mama was not one to invite a pony inside.

"Miss Simmons led Top in," Papa explained. "When Missus Friesen ordered the pony outside, your teacher wouldn't hear of it."

Anna's gaze went to Miss Simmons. She was bent over, helping Carolina and Sally Lil take off their boots. William, George, and Karl were telling all the little Friesens about the roof blowing off. Mrs. Friesen was stirring something on the stove. Ida had changed into a dry shift. Now she was helping Eloise and Ruth out of their wet outer clothes.

"Everyone's all right?" Anna asked, amazed.

"A few cases of frostnip," Mr. Friesen said. He was holding an armful of stiff coats. "Thank the Lord we found you when we did. You weren't more than three rods from the house. But in this weather… " He shuddered. "The children tell me you led them from the school, Anna. You did a fine job."

"Not me. *Top.* Top knew where to go. He led us to the house." Unknotting the shawl, she hurried over to the pony. His coat was matted and wet, snow clung to his feathers, and his mane hung in icy strings.

"You are a sight." She hugged him hard. "When we get home, I promise to give you a good brushing." She lowered her voice. "And a measure of corn. Only don't tell Papa."

"Anna?"

Anna turned to see Miss Simmons coming around the stove toward her.

"Is your pony all right?"

"Yes'm. Thank you for inviting him inside. Though I doubt Missus Friesen's too happy."

"It's the least I could do." Reaching out, Miss Simmons gingerly patted the pony. "You and Top saved our lives."

Anna flushed. She took off her shawl and draped it over a kitchen chair. "Not me, ma'am. It was Top. He led us through the storm. I just hung on."

Miss Simmons frowned, and Anna fidgeted, wondering what she'd done wrong this time.

"Now you listen to me, young lady," Miss Simmons said firmly. "You and Top led us through the storm. You and Top saved our lives." Her frown softened. *"You,* Anna Vail, are one of the bravest girls I know."

Anna blinked at her teacher, not sure why all the praise. "Thank you, Miss Simmons. Only there wasn't nothing brave about it. It's like tending sheep. Top and

I knew we had to get the flock to safety."

Miss Simmons smiled. "You did that. And I thank you."

Embarrassed, Anna flushed harder. She'd never heard so many thank-yous in all her life. She nodded to the other side of the room. "Don't forget to thank Ida and John Jacob and, well, everybody. They were all brave. Even Carolina and Eloise."

Anna looked at Eloise, who was inspecting one of Ida's dry sweaters like it might have lice. "Well, maybe not Eloise," she added under her breath. Just then Sally Lil ran over and flung her arms around Anna's waist. She held tightly, not saying a word, until finally Anna had to pry away her arms. "Goodness, Sally Lil. What's that all about?"

"That's for saving us," Sally Lil replied, her cropped hair sticking up in wet spikes. "Even Eloise said you're a hero."

Anna's brows rose in doubtful surprise and then she shook her head. "You were just as brave, Sally Lil, for holding onto Carolina so she wouldn't fall off Top."

Sally Lil's lips parted in a gasp. "I was brave, wasn't I?" she exclaimed before skipping back to the other girls.

Anna turned to her teacher, who'd slumped on to

the kitchen chair. "And you were brave, too, Miss Simmons! Especially for a schoolmarm from back East."

"Thank you. I hold your opinion in fine regard."

Anna ran her hand down Top's mane, plucking off icicles. "Um, I hope this blizzard won't chase you back to Boston," she added quietly. "Folks round here will rebuild the school in no time. And we'll still need a fine teacher like you."

Miss Simmons sighed. Anna peeked over at her. The teacher's cheeks were streaked with soot. Her skirt was stained from the melting snow. Her hair looked like a tangled skein of wool.

Absently, Miss Simmons tucked a strand back into her bun. "I must say, today was a trying one. Snakes, spiders, storms. That's a lot for a lady from Boston to handle."

Anna's shoulders fell.

"So if I stay, I'll need help."

"If you stay?" Anna repeated, her eyes widening.

Miss Simmons nodded. "Despite today's hardships, I think we learned many important lessons. And isn't that what school's all about? So how about we make a promise to each other, Anna."

"What kind of promise?"

"If you promise to keep coming to learn, I'll promise to keep coming to teach."

Anna scrunched her face as she pondered Miss Simmons's promise.

The teacher crossed her arms. "It's the only way, Anna. I can't handle rattlers and blizzards without Top's and your help."

"Well, in that case, I guess I have no choice," Anna said. "Me and Top promise to keep coming. I know the others would hate to see the school close down." She patted the pony. "Is that all right with you, Top?" she asked, but he was too busy crunching hay to reply.

"At least I'll come on days the sheep don't need tending," Anna added quickly.

"Then it's a deal." Miss Simmons tilted her head. "I can learn a lot about the prairie from you, Anna Vail. And you know, a little book learning could help a sheepherder like you."

Anna shrugged. "Yeah, I reckon it couldn't hurt. I can use arithmetic to keep track of my flock." Then she grinned. "And who knows, one day knowing all the names of the presidents of Nebraska might just come in handy."

LIKE ANNA, ALISON HART grew up on horseback and rode her first pony, Ted, bareback. But she's never tried to herd sheep or ride in a snowstorm! Hart says she loves to write historical fiction because of the way history has shaped our lives today. She is the author of many books for young readers, including SHADOW HORSE, which was nominated for the Edgar Allen Poe Award for Best Children's Mystery.

Hart lives in Virginia with her husband, two kids, two dogs, three horses, and one spoiled guinea pig. She teaches English and creative writing at Blue Ridge Community College in the Shenandoah Valley.

More About Life on the Prairie in the 1880s

Surviving the Children's Blizzard

On January 12, 1888, a storm struck the Great Plains. Homesteaders and ranchers were used to snowstorms, but they were not prepared for this. The weather that morning was mild and sunny. Many children, like Anna and John Jacob, had gone to school as usual. Then, without warning, clouds covered the sun and it began to snow. The warm air turned icy. Bitter winds whipped the snow and soil into a blinding fury, making it impossible to see. During the day, the temperature dropped quickly. In some places it dropped over 70 degrees. By evening it was 40 degrees below zero!

Nebraskans named this terrible storm "The Schoolchildren's Blizzard." Like Anna and her friends, many children were trapped at school when the storm hit. Some children and teachers tried to get home. They found their way through the blinding snow by following rows of cornstalks and fence lines. Others survived by tunneling in

Schoolchildren on the prairie

haystacks or hiding beneath overturned sleds. Tragically, hundreds of settlers died during the blizzard.

Anna and her pony Top Hat are fictional heroes of the great blizzard. But there were many stories of real survivors and their brave deeds. One well-known story is about Minnie May Freeman. Like Anna's teacher Miss Simmons, Miss Freeman taught in a sod schoolhouse. When the storm ripped the tarpaper roof off the school, Minnie tied her pupils together with rope. She led them through the snow to a nearby farmhouse. She became so famous that a song was written about her called "Thirteen Were Saved, or Nebraska's Fearless Maid."

ENDURING EVERYDAY HARDSHIPS

Homesteaders on the prairie braved more than storms. Most homesteaders were poor, and everyday life was hard.

All year long the wind blew constantly. In the summer, the sun scorched the land and grasshoppers ate the crops. In

"Prairie coal"

the bitter winter temperatures, settlers often suffered frozen fingers and toes. Livestock ranging on the prairie froze to death during the severe snowstorms.

Wood was scarce on the plains. Yet homesteaders needed fires in their stoves to cook and keep warm. They had to find other forms of fuel. They learned to burn corncobs, sunflower stalks, and weeds. They discovered that buffalo and cow chips made good fires. The homesteaders called these dried patties of animal dung "prairie coal."

BUILDING SOD HOUSES

Because the prairie lacked trees and lumber was expensive to transport, most homesteaders could not build houses of wood. They adopted the local Native American custom of building with sod, the thick top layer of the grass-covered soil. To construct houses and schools, the settlers cut the sod into fifty-pound blocks one foot wide, two feet long, and four inches thick. The tough roots of the prairie grass held the soil in the blocks tightly together. Settlers made walls by laying the blocks grassy side down and stacking them like bricks. It took about an acre of land to cut enough blocks for a small sod house. Then the homesteaders added roofs by placing a row of cottonwood poles across the top of the walls and laying tarpaper or sod over the poles.

Sod house

Soddies were warm in winter and cool in summer, and they wouldn't burn in a prairie fire. But they leaked when it rained and dirt fell from the walls and ceilings. The floors

Prairie girl

were hard-packed dirt, so nothing ever stayed clean. Soddies were also homes to mice, reptiles, bedbugs, fleas, flies, and lice. "We all took baths with plenty of sheep dip in the water," Sarah Olds, a Nevada homesteader wrote about rooting out fleas and lice. "I boiled all our clothes in sheep dip and kerosene."

LIVING ON A PRAIRIE FARM

Chores on a farm were never ending. Children as young as six years old milked cows, collected eggs, hauled water, tended sheep, and fed the stove. Five-year-old Grace McCance herded cattle all day, alone on the prairie. In the spring and summer, crops needed to be planted and harvested, weeded and watered. That meant children only attended school from October to May. Like Eugene, many only attended school when it was an "off day" on the family farm.

GOING TO SCHOOL

To most children, school was a welcome relief from chores. The school was often miles away, and children arrived on foot, on horseback, and in buggies. Laura Ingalls Wilder's daughter Rose rode her donkey, Spookendyke, to school. Some students brought their

A McGuffey's Reader

own slates and writing tablets. Some also brought Bibles, magazines, and McGuffey's Readers carefully covered with oilcloth wrappers to share with their classmates. All students brought their lunches. Rose Wilder brought an apple and slices of brown bread spread with bacon grease because "we were too poor to have butter."

Anna and her friends were lucky to get a kind, educated teacher like Miss Simmons. Many teachers were as young as sixteen and seventeen years old. Many had no experience. They worked for little pay: thirty-five dollars a month or ten dollars

Inside a sod schoolhouse

with room and board. Anna and her friends were also lucky to have a blackboard, ink, and pens. Many teachers and students had to write on old packing papers or in the dirt floor of the school.

PLAYTIME ON THE PRAIRIE

Despite the chores and hardships, children living on the prairie did have fun. At school, they played baseball or entertained themselves with group games called Snap the Whip, Red Rover, and Run Sheep Run. When it snowed, they built forts, made snowmen, and skated on the frozen river.

A popular board game of the time

Indoors, they played checkers, chess, dominoes, and card games like Old Maid and Our Birds. Adults encouraged kids to play board games such as Errand Boy and Mansion of Happiness because they taught "lessons," for example, the importance of working hard and being honest.

Children used their imaginations to have fun as well. Grace McCance tells about tying strings to tumbleweeds and riding them like horses. Other playful activities included swimming in water troughs, making dolls from cornhusks, building playhouses from buffalo bones, and weaving flowers into necklaces.

Prairie children also loved their pets. Eliza McAuley had a pet antelope named Jennie who "came bounding to me and followed me home." Like Anna, Virginia Reed loved her pony, Billy. "How I enjoyed riding my pony, galloping over the plain gathering wildflowers!" Grace McCance adored her red heifer calf. "She was an odd-looking beast, I know, but to me she was beautiful. I named her Bess and loved her all my life."

A doll made from corn husks

Most children growing up on the prairie did not feel that their lives were tough. Rattlesnakes, grasshopper plagues, and thunderstorms were adventures, not hardships. Like Anna, they loved their sod homes on the wild, grassy plains.

In 1888...

❋ Women could not vote! It would be thirty-one more years (1919) before women could vote for the President of the United States.

❋ There were two terrible blizzards. From March 11 to March 14, forty to fifty inches of snow fell on the East Coast from Maryland to Maine. Winds blew up to 48 miles per hour, causing snowdrifts forty to fifty feet high. More than 400 deaths were attributed to the "Great White Hurricane," as it was later named.

Alcott

Twain

❋ Kids were reading *Little Women* by Louisa May Alcott and *The Adventures of Tom Sawyer* by Mark Twain—books that are still popular today.

❋ Christmas was also an important celebration. Even homesteaders living in the poorest of soddies made the most of the day. A wild plum bush or tumbleweed might be decorated with paper chains and strings of popcorn. A stocking might hold an orange and some nuts. "Mother made our Christmas gifts," a child recalls. "A matchbox covered with pretty paper and decorated with pictures from the seed catalog was one of my treasured gifts."

❄ Folks were drinking Coca-Cola! The syrup for the drink was invented in 1886 and sold for five cents a glass as a soda fountain drink. Its popularity increased when "bubbles" (carbonated water) were added to make it "delicious and refreshing."

❄ ❄ ❄ ❄ ❄ ❄ ❄ ❄

AUTHOR'S NOTE

The quote about living in a sod home came from *Twenty Miles from a Match: Homesteading in Western Nevada* by Sarah E. Olds (University of Nevada Press, 1978). The quote from Grace McCance came from Andrea Warren's book *Pioneer Girl: Growing up on the Prairie.* The quote from Virginia Reed came from *Words West.* The quote from Eliza McAuley came from *Settler's Children: Growing up on the Great Plains* by Elizabeth Hampsten (University of Oklahoma Press). The quote from Rose Wilder came from *Growing Up in Pioneer America* by Judith Pinkerton Josephson.

To Learn More About the Homesteaders

BOOKS:

Freedman, Russell. *Children of the Wild West*. Clarion Books, New York: 1983.

Gintzler, A. S. *Rough and Ready Homesteaders*. John Muir Publications, New Mexico: 1994.

Graves, Kerry A. *Going to School in Pioneer Times*. Capstone Press, Minnesota: 2002.

Murphy, Jim. *Dear America: My Face to the Wind. The Diary of Sarah Jane Price, a Prairie Teacher*. Scholastic, Inc. New York: 2001.

Josephson, Judith Pinkerton. *Growing Up in Pioneer America*. Lerner Publications, Minneapolis: 2003.

Kalman, Bobbie. *Games from Long Ago*. Crabtree Publishing, New York: 1995.

Patent, Dorothy Hinshaw. *Homesteading: Settling America's Heartland*. Walker and Company, New York: 1998.

Warren, Andrea. *Pioneer Girl: Growing up on the Prairie*. Morrow Junior Books, New York: 1998.

WEBSITES: *www.museumoftheamericanwest.org; www.nebraskastudies.org; www.okprairie.com*

The following sources were also helpful in my research:
Frontier Children by Linda Peavy and Ursula Smith (University of Oklahoma Press, 1999), *Buffalo Gals: Women of the Old West* by Brandon Marie Miller (Lerner Publications, 1995), *History of Nebraska* by James C. Olson (Bison Books, 3rd Edition, 1997), and *Words West* by Ginger Wadsworth (Clarion Books, 2003).